The Man Who Saved Two Notch

by

R.W. Ridley

I0571835

Middlebury House Publishing
Copyright © 2011 R.W Ridley

ISBN-10 097920674X
ISBN-13 9780979206740

Printed in the United States of America

For the yellow finch

Mean's what works in these times.
-   John Arnaught

Preface

I was there. I seen him die. The whore and him faced down nearly ten men. The sun was buried deep under the curve of the earth by the time the first shot was fired. Clouds smothered the tiny white slit of a moon. The flashes popping out of the muzzles of their guns lit up the night. The crack of the gunshots echoed through the emptiness of the world around us. If you listened hard enough, you could pick up the sounds of dying men fighting for their last breaths. But I didn't care to listen for that sort of thing.

When the dust settled and I was sure it was over, I approached the toppled mountain of a man. His feet was still moving, flexing up and down. Blood was pouring from all his wounds, old and new. His eyes were darting left and right. Words were coming out of his mouth, but I couldn't make heads or tails out of what he was saying.

I knelt down and turned my ear towards his mouth.

"There's a lot of 'em." That's what I could make out anyway. It came out in a pile of mumbling. I looked where his darting eyes was scanning and noticed the clouds had give way. He was lying under a star-speckled sky.

"Yes, sir," I said.

He reached up and grabbed hold of the back of my head. "Feel bad about the little ones."

"Sir?" I struggled to work myself free, but his grip was strong as granite.

"Henry?"

"Yes, sir?"

"I've gotta answer for the little ones." He chuckled. "I ain't sure they all deserved it."

That's when I knew he wasn't talking about the stars. I didn't know what to say, so I just said, "S'pose that'll be worked out soon enough."

He smiled. "That's what I'm afraid of."

A couple of minutes later he spoke his last words. The bouncing of his eyes come to a stop and he fixed them on me. "Don't let that fucking bear eat me."

1

I ran with the Devil once, thanks to miserable Old Kelly. His name was Abel Decker, and most folks only know him as a legend. God help me, I knew him as a man.

Old Kelly was the rector of our town, Two Notch. She was gloomy and ugly in spirit and appearance, but she possessed the gift of communication with the good Lord above, so she had a hold over the town. If you could even call Two Notch that at the time. It wasn't much more than a carcass of a town thanks to the war.

I was on the short side of twelve when I got the calling to find Abel Decker so he could save the dead streets of Two Notch, and even at my young age I could see that seventy-five years of war brings nothing but collapse and endless misery. War takes most everything that matters, people included.

What it leaves behind is a wasteland of a country. Hell, it might not even be a country no more. Can't nobody say for sure. Mostly cause don't nobody know who to ask. What we've got is a shit-bowl of towns scattered from one dusty expanse of land to the next. Decaying buildings. Crumbling pavement. Rusted out vehicles. No technology, or "modern comforts" to speak of. You may see a motorized moped here and there. And they get electricity going every now and again, but it never lasts very long. The old ones in Two Notch talk about times before when near everything was run by electricity. They still drone on about talking to folks on devices no bigger than a small chip of wood and sending pictures and something called video through the air. Hell, I ain't even sure how they made pictures. None of it made a lick of sense to me.

'Bout the only thing that makes sense to me then and now is living a life of misery in shitty old Two Notch. As wretched as it was and is, it's all I know, all I cared to know back then. I was happy scraping out my day to days with my Pa, not knowing what went on a mile past any of the roads in and out of my little dead town.

Would have spent the rest of my life that way if it wasn't for Old Kelly and her goddamn visions. Yep, if it wasn't for her, I never would have set out on the path to meet up with the Devil himself.

2

It was fuck-all luck they sent me to fetch Decker because my Pa hadn't broken down and butchered our riding pony for meat when everyone else had. The old man's back broke in the war, and he couldn't do none of the clearing on our land by hand. He needed old Runner to pull up roots and boulders that most men could dig up with little effort. I never really knew why he thought it was so important to clear everything away. The land was shit for growing even the foulest weeds.

"Soil's got yield left, boy," he'd say. "You'll see."

"What's yield?"

"Means it's got nutrients. Food for plants. Big beautiful plants."

I looked at the hard crusty ground and tried my best not to laugh at him. "Mr. Brindle says it's used up. Says you can't grow a blade of grass for thousands of square miles. He says he suspects the whole planet is dead as Two Notch."

"Brindle's a red-faced fool. Two Notch ain't dead."

"It ain't?"

"We live in Two Notch, don't we?"

"Yes, sir."

"We dead?"

"No, sir."

"The other folks you see walking the streets of Two Notch dead?"

"No, sir, not the ones I talk to anyway. Can't say for sure on the others."

"Well, take my word, they ain't. As long as Two Notch has got people, it ain't dead. The same goes for the rest of the planet, too. You've got my permission to punch Brindle in his cake hole next time he says something like that."

"Don't reckon I'll do that," I said. "He ain't the most tolerable person in Two Notch as it is. If I punch him in the cake hole, he's bound to be a lot less tolerable."

Pa flashed a yellow-toothed grin. "You're pretty smart for a kid, Henry Francis Arnaught. Your Ma would be proud."

Ma was dead. Died before I can remember. She was a small woman, dark hair, pretty as the air is dry. Married my old man before he went off to fight in the war. Tried to get pregnant so she wouldn't have to serve, but a baby never took hold. Pa served his tour until he broke his back. The military folks plopped him down on his sick bed at home and then served Ma with her orders to ship out in six weeks. She commenced to trying to have a baby with Pa the second those army fellas left the house. She didn't care if he had a broken back. It almost killed the old man to hear him tell it. They worked on baby making night and day. Pa said it felt like someone was digging a knife in his back every time they took to doing it.

Two-weeks before she was to catch a transport to basic training, I found my spot in her belly and they released her from military service.

"Came this close to calling you 'exempt from service,'" Pa used to say holding his index finger a half-inch from his thumb. "But Old Kelly's got a rule 'bout only using Christian names."

"Well," I said, "least that's something I can thank her for."

Ma died into my first year on this planet. Took to coughing and pissing blood. Since all the doctors were gone, no one knew what her sickness was. They treated her like they treated everyone who can't contribute to the welfare of the community. Cut off her share of water rations. Give her bones to suck on instead of meat. Although Pa tried to get her to eat his. She took portions for a day or two, but by day three she couldn't hold down a good spit much less a chunk of meat. From her first cough to her last breath no more than four weeks went by.

There was a funeral. All the people who refused to care for her or give her extra water, attended.

"Bunch of heartless bastards," Pa said. "All the women cried their eyes out and tried to get me to take up with one of their daughters. One girl was barely older than you."

"Who?"

"Not important. I was sickened by the offers. Them old bags wanted in on what's mine and yours and they were selling their daughters to get it."

"But we ain't got nothing."

"No one's got nothing around here. But we got less nothing than most folks."

This is how most our conversations went about the folks of Two Notch. Pa didn't have a use for none of them, but he tolerated them because we all needed each other for survival. And the folks tolerated him because he done his time in the war. He come back useless, but at least he fought for them. They honored that as much as dishonorable people could.

Old Kelly kept the scriptures and interpreted messages from the higher power and pretty much set the law for Two Notch. I'm not sure how she got her position, but no one disputed her authority. She even had her own gaggle of goons who kept her law. They were the healthiest among us. Got extra rations for their service and had their run of the town.

Old Kelly called a meeting one cold morning and made her announcement to everyone in front of the rundown town hall. She stood on the steps with her goons on either side of her and said with a wheeze, "Fucking marauders are headed this way."

This set off a series of discussions among the gathered.

"Shut up!" Old Kelly said with her hand raised.

"How do you know?" someone dared to ask. Whoever it was, was lucky Old Kelly didn't recognize his voice 'cause she would have had her goons work him over for asking such a question.

"God told me, you idiot. Ain't we established that beyond a shadow of a doubt yet? God lays words on my ears! Damn it. I don't want to have to explain how this works to you people every fucking time I call you together. I'm a goddamned prophet!"

The crowd went silent.

"These marauders are coming for our young."

This was a fact that I must admit made me a tad more uneasy than the usual bad news made me feel.

"How can we stop them?"

"We can't," Old Kelly said. "We need help. God told me to send for Abel Decker."

A collective gasp rose up from the crowd.

"Decker's the devil himself," a voice from the crowd said.

"That may be true," Old Kelly said, "but he works for hire. We'll pay him for his services."

"With what?"

"Whatever we got, water, meat, women or men if he prefers."

"Can we vote on this?" An unknown male voice asked.

"Who said that?"

No one confessed.

"We vote on shit. God tells me what to do, and I tell you what to do. That's the arrangement we agreed on. Or am I misremembering, 'cause I can get my boys to commence with renegotiating our agreement?"

There was no answer from the crowd.

"Fine. Arnaught?"

My father stepped forward. "Yeah, Kelly."

"Can you ride that pony of yours?"

"Not very far."

"Your boy?"

"He can ride, but I won't let him."

"Then lend your pony to someone who can."

Pa hesitated. "I'm afraid that wouldn't be wise on my part."

Kelly raised a bushy eyebrow. "And why not?"

"'Cause everyone else has butchered their livestock for meat. I need my pony for work. I let him fall in the hands of someone who's hungry, they'll butcher him before they reach the city limits. Don't matter what you say. Hungry is hungry."

"Not my concern. I'll let you choose someone you can trust, but you will give up your pony for this, am I understood?"

Pa nodded. He turned to the crowd and examined all the emaciated faces. His eyes fell on me. "My boy will go," he said. "But not alone."

"Can't spare more than one body…"

"Someone will accompany him, or I'll put an axe in the pony's head soon as I get home."

Kelly fumed. She didn't liked being challenged, but she didn't want to be impertinent toward my father either. She was feared by the crowd, but he was respected. "Then choose from the infirm. Can't waste two able-bodied souls on this mission."

"I can go by myself, Pa."

"You can't. I won't have it. You need an extra pair of eyes and ears out there. Lord knows what's past the canyon."

He was talking about Besser Canyon. It was between Two Notch and Abel Decker, and it was fine to travel by day, but once night fell… well, it ain't prudent to be caught without sunlight in Besser Canyon, let's just say that. If half the rumors and stories are true about the things that have happened to poor souls traveling Besser under the stars, I'd rather take my chances with the fucking marauders.

Sandy Slater stepped to the front of the crowd. "Do we get compensation?"

"How's that?" Old Kelly asked.

"If'n I volunteer my Doreen to go with the Arnaught boy, do I get compensated?"

Old Kelly picked her brown teeth. "What'd you have in mind?"

"Extra shares."

"Of what?"

"Water, meat, wood. I'd be giving up a child. That should be good for something more than a pat on the back."

Old Kelly thought about her request. "You can keep your child's share until she comes back."

"And if she don't come back?"

"Half her share for the next year."

Sandy Slater smiled. "Doreen is volunteered."

Old Kelly looked the homely young girl over. "What's her feebleness? I done said I can't afford to lose two able-bodied youngsters."

"She's slow-witted," Sandy Slater said pushing the girl forward.

Old Kelly hacked a laugh out of her throat. "Slow-witted ain't feeble enough. Two-thirds of your townsfolk would forget to breathe if it weren't automatic."

"She pees herself. Often."

"Hell, I pee myself twice a day."

"She was born without a vessel."

Old Kelly stiffened at this news. She leaned forward. "How do you know she was born without a vessel?"

"Birthing doctor said so. Girl's insides is all twisted."

"How long you known this?"

"She came to us this way. She's my sister Carla's girl. We lost her to cancer a few months back. It was Carla's confession before she got took."

"And you're just now coming forward?"

"We were fond of my sister. She'd asked us to keep her. By law, we're obliged to take on our blood's burdens."

Old Kelly nodded. "That is true, but by law, you're also obliged to turn in the names of females who can't reproduce."

"It is not our fault, Old Kelly. My sister bore the child. It was her responsibility to make the report. We only just got the child. We assumed she had followed the law."

"I have no reports of infertile females among us." Old Kelly waved the girl forward. Doreen, no older than eight, sauntered toward her. "She is a purposeless child. She should have been put down."

"She has a purpose now," Pa said.

Old Kelly patted the infertile girl on the head. "God does not see her good fortune this way. She has been spared by dumb luck. The fact that she can assist your boy is not divine in any way. I would know it."

"Nevertheless, she is the perfect companion for Henry on his journey."

Old Kelly nodded. "She is that."

"Then she goes," Sandy Slater said. "And we get her rations."

"She goes," Old Kelly said pushing the child back. "But you do not get her rations."

"But you said…"

"That's when I thought you were sacrificing something that had worth. A half-wit female that cannot reproduce is no sacrifice. You're lucky we don't throw you in jail for wasting rations on her."

"But she is not my child…"

"So you say," Old Kelly said. "You are rid of her now. If she returns, she will be dealt with as the law dictates."

Doreen walked over and grabbed my hand. It startled me, and I yanked my hand away from hers. But a stern look from Pa caused me to reach back and squeeze it tight.

Old Kelly looked at me with her yellow eyes. "You're on God's journey, boy. He will watch over you. Sacrifice the girl if you have to along the way, but whatever you do, make it to Decker and let him know the fucking marauders are coming."

"Yes, ma'am."

"Use them words exactly."

"Yes, ma'am."

"We'll be giving you a canteen with near eight ounces of water."

"Yes, ma'am."

"Now, just 'cause you got eight ounces don't mean you got to consume it all."

"Yes, ma'am."

"As an incentive, I've instructed the town treasure to set aside eight gold pieces for you. You'll get a gold piece for every ounce you don't drink. Understood?"

"Yes, ma'am. What about Doreen?"

"What about her?"

"Don't she get a canteen?"

"She don't."

Pa stepped forward. "That ain't right. You gotta give the girl a canteen."

"God did not instruct me to."

"But she'll die without her own, and I know my boy, he'll give up every last drop of his to nourish her along the way."

Old Kelly scowled. "He won't."

"He will."

"He won't because if it's found out that he give a drop to the girl, you will owe me two gold pieces for every ounce he doesn't bring back."

"How can you know if he shares it with her?"

"First, if she returns alive I will know he shared water rations with her. Second, God will tell me."

"So, the girl is being sent to die?"

"The girl is being sent because you requested the boy have a companion. Her death is on your head."

I recognized the look on Pa's face. He wanted to throw his fist into Old Kelly's face and drive her big bottomed frame to the ground with a crunching thud, but he'd be tried for treason and sentenced to hang before she hit the ground. Doreen must have sensed his mood, too because she reached up and grabbed his hand. The three of us departed the others.

"Leave at day break," Old Kelly said as we made our way through the street. "No later. We haven't much time. My top man will accompany you to Besser Pass. Once you get through the pass, head dead East. You'll find Abel Decker."

3

Doreen come home with us. Her aunt tried to argue that we owed her rations for taking her, but Pa wasn't having any of it. He called her an idiot and a bunch of other names I wasn't that familiar with, and Pa would have been mad at me if I was.

We set around a fire outside the house that night and cooked a couple of rattlers. They were skinny, even for snakes. Got less than ¼ pound of edible meat between them. Pa let me and Doreen have most of it.

"You know him, Pa?" I asked sucking a pinch of fat off a bone.

"Who?"

"Abel Decker."

He stoked the flames with a fire iron. "Know of him. He served while I did. Never crossed paths, but I heard plenty of stories about him."

"I heard he's mean."

"Well, he is that. That's why Old Kelly wants him. Mean's what works in these times. He served more tours in the war than anyone else, thirty-two from what I remember."

"Heard he wiped out entire villages, children included."

"Wouldn't surprise me. That's what you do in war."

His reply gave me pause. "Did you?"

He stared deep into the fire. "We don't talk about my time. You know that."

I nodded. "Jacob Taye says Decker likes killing kids. Says he still takes up the practice from time to time."

"Jacob Taye's been beat down by his old man one too many times. A man don't ever take to a thing like that. No man in his right mind, anyway."

"Maybe Decker ain't in his right mind."

"Maybe he ain't, but you've got nothing to worry about. You're bringing him work. He's likely to thank you for it. Old Kelly's prepared to give him a barrel of water and three women of his choice for his services. You be sure to tell him that right off."

"Yes, sir."

Pa reached down behind the log he was sitting on and pulled up his old service weapon. "This here is a modified Pulse-3 AR-15 Army assault rifle. You got three 30-round magazines for killing and, fully charged, you've got 16 electromagnetic pulse shots that will render your enemy immobile for 45 seconds." He held up a round plastic box the size of a watch face. "This is your battery. You'll have two. Don't put the battery in until you absolutely have to because the battery begins draining the second you put it in." He held up the rifle and pointed to the two triggers. "The red trigger is ammo. The blue trigger is the pulse. Understand?"

"Yes, sir."

"Let me hear you say it."

"Red is for ammo. Blue is for pulse."

"Good. I want you to say that to yourself over and over again whenever you notice the quiet because the quiet is when they'll come."

"They?"

"The things in this world that want to kill you."

I swallowed the dryness in my throat, and it hurt.

"If you can, greet Decker with a battery loaded. He makes a move on you, pull the blue trigger and hightail it out of there."

I nodded with a blank look.

"He comes at you again, pull the red trigger and hope you hit your target, 'cause if he comes at you again you're out of triggers."

I turned away from him hoping he'd take the hint that I was tired of talking about Decker and triggers and things that wanted to kill me. I cast my eyes on Doreen who was sucking on some snake meat. She hadn't said a word the entire time I had come to know her.

"She must really be simple," I said.

She didn't acknowledge hearing me at all.

"She's quiet," Pa said, "but quiet don't make you simple."

"Don't see why I got to take her with me."

"You need another set of eyes and ears out there."

I shook my head. "Just 'cause she's got 'em don't mean they're any use to me."

"Even so, I'd feel better if you had someone with you."

Doreen stuffed the last morsel of meat in her mouth and looked up at us. She had grease caked around her lips. Without warning, she let out a loud belch.

Pa snorted. "Well, looks like her gas reflexes are in order."

I laughed in spite of myself. I was torn between resenting having to take her with me, and being relieved that I wouldn't be going alone. If all she could do is work up a cold, uninviting stare and thunderous burps, it didn't seem hardly worth it to bring her along.

Pa and I continued to jaw around the fire while Doreen eventually dosed off. She curled up in the fetal position by Pa's feet and drifted off to la-la land. She looked peaceful as a newborn. The more I looked at her the sleepier I got. Pa kicked dirt on the fire and scooped her up in his arms.

"Little bit's got the right idea. You need your rest, too."

With that, we headed into the house. I was asleep the second I hit our skanky old mattress.

4

The next morning, Pa grabbed his breakfast rations for the next three days and forced me and Doreen to fill our guts with as much food as we could eat. We lapped it up like it was our last meal.

"The both of you got a responsibility to the other," Pa said. "You watch each other. Don't go wondering off out of site of one another. Understand?"

I thought it over. "Even when we're doing nature's business?"

"Especially when you're doing nature's business. Never is a man more vulnerable than when he is evacuating his plumbing."

I squished my face in disgust. I had no interest in watching Doreen evacuate her plumbing, and I hoped she didn't want to see me doing the same.

"Now is not the time for modesty, Henry Arnaught."

"Yes, sir."

He reached out and took my hand. "I'm going to tell you something your Ma used to say."

I nodded anxiously because I cherished the moments he talked about my mother the most.

"God places the heaviest burden on those who can carry its weight," he said. "That there's a quote from a man who used to play football. Reggie White. Your Ma didn't know a thing about the game or Reggie White, but she knew that quote. Carried it with her on a piece of paper. I buried her with it because I don't have any use for God nor people who put too much stock into him, outside of your Ma. But it meant something to her, and I suppose I wouldn't mind if it meant something to you."

I chomped down on a dry biscuit with sugar sprinkled across the top. Mid-chew I asked, "What's football?"

He smiled. "It's a thing people used to play when people didn't have to worry about much other than putting up with bullshit at work and home. When surviving became an hourly endeavor, we all stopped caring about it and any other games they used to have for our entertainment."

"Did you play?"

"Not very well."

A man's voice came from the front yard, "Arnaught, it's time to depart!"

"It ain't time!" My old man yelled.

"Old Kelly says it is."

Pa moved down the hallway to the front door and peeked through the window to see who she had sent.

"Buster Darnell. Man's got the brain of a flea and the body of bloated pig. Best man, my fat ass." Pa walked back to the kitchen.

Doreen covered her mouth with her hand and snickered.

Pa turned to her. "What's got her all giggly?"

I swallowed the last of the biscuit. "I think she's laughing 'cause you said something about your fat ass."

"C'mon, Arnaught! Old Kelly will have my nuts if I don't get your boy and that little barren girl to Besser Pass soon as possible!"

Pa gritted his teeth. "Hold your sack! They'll be out in two shakes!"

I pushed back from the table and stood.

"Don't waste the food. Put it in Runner's saddlebag."

"Yes sir."

"I holstered the gun to his saddle already. The ammo's packed. There's two bedrolls and I stitched up a couple of red fox ponchos. They won't keep you dry, but they'll keep you warm... somewhat, anyway."

"Yes, sir."

He knelt down. "They're this thing that people do... I ain't never showed you because... I ain't sure why I've never showed you, to tell you the truth. But I'll show you now."

"What is it?"

"It's called a hug. Your Ma was good at it." He spread his arms open wide.

I stood there not knowing what my part was in a hug.

"Come here."

I approached him slowly. When I got within arms' length, he grabbed me and pulled me into his body. "I wish to all hell that I wasn't a useless man. A father shouldn't have to send his boy to do man's work."

"I ain't a boy," I said even though I didn't believe it.

"You're my boy, Henry." He patted me on the back and released me.

I stepped back from the hug, examined his wet cheeks, and noticed a lump developing in my throat.

Without warning, Doreen strolled up and pressed herself against my old man's chest. He looked at first horrified, then confused and finally pleased. He hugged her, too.

"Arnaught! Don't make me come in there!"

"Go out back and bring Runner to the front of the house," Pa said standing with Doreen in his arms.

I took off in a sprint toward the back before he could turn to open the front door.

Pa and Buster Darnell were in a heated argument when I rode Runner around the house. The skinny pony snorted and dug into the ground with its front hooves when I first mounted him. He didn't like riders, even riders as puny as me, but he wasn't spirited enough to throw me. I gave him a gentle kick in the ribs, and he moved without a fuss.

"Old Kelly said eight ounces of water," Pa said holding the canteen. Doreen was looking up at the two men with an awkward smile.

"There're eight ounces in there."

Pa shook the canteen. "Bullshit!"

"Don't see how you can tell a thing like that by just shaking the canteen."

"'Cause when you ain't got a lot of something, you know what the least little bit sounds like."

Buster tilted his head to the left and studied Pa's face. "Okay, I took a swig. But it wasn't but a small one."

Pa didn't hesitate. He slapped Buster across his round face. "They don't go without the full eight ounces."

"There ain't nothing I can do about it now," Buster said rubbing the sting out of his cheek.

Pa held out his hand. "Hand it over."

"Hand what over?"

"Your water rations for the day."

Buster stepped back. "Don't know what you're talking about."

"You work for Old Kelly. You're her top man. I know damn well you get daily rations."

"I get weekly like everyone else," Buster said sounding incredulous.

"Buster Darnell, I will knock you to the ground and yank your tongue out of your mouth before you can say 'what for!' I swear it! Now, hand over your dailies."

Buster took a moment to measure Pa. He wasn't sure if a man who broke his back in the war could do such a thing as Pa just threatened. After an uncomfortable amount of time passed, he reached in his coat pocket and pulled out a bag made out of eel skin and held it out.

Pa took it. It sloshed as he shook it.

"That's at least four ounces," Buster said.

"Could be," Pa said.

"That with the canteen is more than eight ounces. Henry won't know what to do with all that water."

"He'll know what to do with it," Pa said handing over the canteen and bag to me.

I reached down and took them. My instinct was to smell the bag. "Stinks."

"It's mud eel," Buster said. "That stank won't never go away."

"I find out you touch any of their rations I'll make good on that threat. Understood?"

Buster nodded. "I'll mind mine and they can mind theirs if'n you do me a favor."

Pa didn't answer he just gave Buster the cock-eye.

"Relax, I just want your word you won't say nothing to Old Kelly about my... brief indiscretion there with the water rations."

Pa nodded.

"You're a good man, Captain Arnaught."

"Don't call me that," Pa said reaching down and picking up Doreen. He hoisted her up on Runner.

I helped her get situated, and she wrapped her arms around my waist. I have never felt so unsettled.

Pa tapped the butt of the gun. "What'd I tell ya'?"

"Red is for ammo and blue is for pulse."

Buster smiled and revealed all three of his teeth. "I'll be damned. An army issue." He reached out to touch it but Pa smacked his hand away.

"What'd you do that for?"

"Because I don't like you," Pa said. He turned his attention to me. "If Buster gets the wrong idea about anything while he's escorting you to Besser Canyon, don't bother with the blue trigger. Go straight for the red."

"Yes, sir."

"Touchy," Buster said walking to the street in front of our house. He mounted an electric moped that had more wear and tear than paint and metal, put a helmet on his melon head, and cranked the tiny engine.

I shook my head. "He's just going to slow us down on that thing. I'd be better off just letting Runner do his thing."

"He's an idiot and that old moped of his is a nuisance, but he'll watch out for you like his life depended on it. You can be sure of that. Old Kelly's right to send him. You'll be rid of him once you get to the pass."

He patted Runner on the rump and the pony stepped toward the street.

I turned in the saddle and gave Pa a smile. "Maybe you can show me that football game when I get back."

Pa nodded. "I wouldn't be opposed to that."

The high pitched putter of the moped filled the air as it rumbled like a lazy turtle over the cracked pavement.

Doreen released me and waved to my old man.

He stuck his hand up and grinned.

5

We were going painfully slow. It even frustrated Runner. Buster had the throttle pulled back all the way on the moped, and it still couldn't go no faster than a brisk walking speed. We tried to stay behind him, but it was just impossible. We were nearly twenty feet in front of him before we even left the town limits.

"Slow down," he yelled over that rubber band engine of his. "God damn it!"

"I'd have to cut Runner's legs off to go any slower," I yelled back.

"I am your escort! Now, I demand you slow down."

"Runner ain't one for following demands." I tapped my heels on Runner's ribs, and he picked up the pace. Doreen giggled.

"I seen that! You're cajoling that bucket of glue to go faster!"

I cupped my hand over my ear. "I can't hear ya'!"

"I said you're making that horse go faster!"

"Go faster?" I turned slightly and whispered, "Hold on," to Doreen. Back to Buster I said,. "Whatever you say, Mr. Darnell!" With that I slapped Runner with the palm of my hand and shouted, "Get up!" Runner bolted forth and ran like he ain't never ran before.

Buster yelled something, but we were too far too fast to be able to make out a thing he was saying. Given the nature of the previous conversation, I imagine he was imploring us to slow down. Doreen and me both shared a good laugh as Runner galloped effortlessly across the dusty terrain.

***

Runner kept up a good pace for the next mile or so, but he eventually slowed to a trot and then a lumbering walk. He didn't have nothing but dried grass and hay in his belly. I stopped at one point and give him some water from the eel skin bag. Pa said not to waste any of my rations on him. He said old Runner would find enough dew in the early mornings to get by, but I couldn't see how that would be possible. There was no way I was drinking anything from that stinky eel skin bag anyway. I poured a little water in my hand and let Runner lap it up. The stank didn't bother him a bit.

Buster was out of sight. If you listened hard enough you could hear that toy engine on that moped of his and him cussing up a storm in the distance. I was hoping he would be too tired to try and punish us for leaving him behind when he finally caught up. My guess was he was sipping on his whiskey rations about as often as he was working up the next curse word to let fly from his fat face.

I held onto Runner's reins and we walked him the next half mile or so. He couldn't tell the difference between us on or off his back. Together, Doreen and me didn't weigh as much as half a full grown man. But I was tired of sitting on Runner's back. My groin was beginning to feel like it had been stretched to its limit.

I couldn't take the silence so I finally asked Doreen, "You talk?"

She shook her head.

"Got something wrong with you?"

She shook her head again.

"Just don't want to?"

She nodded.

I shrugged. "I guess I can see that. You simple?"

She shook her head.

"I'll take your word for it."

We walked a little further without talking. "Don't worry about my water rations. You can have some."

She didn't respond.

"I kind of got used to not having much water anyways. Pa says I'm like a camel. I guess that's good. Don't know for sure, because I ain't 100% positive what a camel is."

She slapped my shoulder and pointed to her back. She hunched over and made a funny face.

"What the hell is wrong with you?"

She continued with her hunched over posture, and made some weird baying noise.

"Oh," I said. "You showing me a camel?"

She nodded.

"Yeah? That's what it looks like?"

She tilted her head to the right and left and frowned to let me know that it was the best she could do.

"Ain't so sure that was a good thing then."

I turned to see if I could catch a glimpse of Buster approaching. Nothing. I saw Doreen mimic what I was doing. "He's way back there. Bound to be mad as hell when he catches up with us. You keep your space when it comes to him. You may not be simple, but he is. He's likely to be irritable and extra stupid."

She bent down and picked up a rock and tossed it from hand to hand.

"Lord, don't throw no rocks at him. That'll make him madder."

She shrugged.

"I'm serious. You ain't got much muscle to put behind it and you're likely to miss, too."

She stopped.

I didn't know that she wasn't walking beside me for a click or two. But when I noticed I stopped and looked at her. "What?"

She pointed to a hill about twenty feet away. There was a spindly little lizard hiked up its hind legs looking at us.

"What of it?"

She reared back and flung the rock with a lot more strength than I gave her credit for. Bam! The rock hit the lizard and blood exploded out in all directions.

"Holy Moses! How in the hell did you do a thing like that?"

She smiled and wiped the dirt from her hands.

"You might not be such a burden on this trip after all."

***

We took up camp at the head of Besser Pass about an hour before dusk. I put Doreen to work. She unsaddled Runner and made sure he was happy. The old horse got on with her pretty good. He liked her better than he liked most people.

I got a fire going. It was a good blaze by the time Buster showed up. He pushed his moped into camp just as the sun dipped its toe into the horizon. Like I expected, he was drunk. His considerable lack of overall fitness had him breathing like he'd run like the dickens to get there. He pushed his moped to the ground and flopped down on his back next to the fire. He was breathing so hard I started making plans for his burial in my mind.

"You dumb-ass kids is lucky I'm a forgiving man."

"You okay?"

"I'm…" He swallowed and then had a coughing fit. "I'm goddamn Superman."

I looked at Doreen and rolled my eyes. She giggled.

Buster cocked his head toward her. "You think that's funny?"

"She don't mean nothing by it. She's just simple that's all."

Buster hacked a loogie and spat it onto the fire. "I got every right to give you a bona fide beaten for going on ahead like that."

"You was going too slow," I said.

"I was going the right amount. That's what I was going because I am the A-dult." He put extra emphasis on the 'A' as if not doing so would make us equals.

"Well, Runner's an A-dult, too, and he saw fit to get on his gallop."

He lifted his hand weakly and pointed a crooked finger at me. "I ain't stupid, boy. I seen you urging him on."

"Sun was in your eyes. You didn't see nothing."

He sat up on his elbows. "Don't test me."

"Just trying to set things straight," I said doing my best to not look intimidated.

He gave me the evil eye and then shouted, "Simple girl!"

Doreen looked at me before stepping away from Runner and approached Buster.

"Fetch me my spirit rations from my steed."

Doreen looked at him blankly.

"Go on."

She didn't move.

"What's wrong with her?"

I shrugged. "I don't know. She probably don't know what you mean by steed."

He chuckled. "Lord, she is simple. My moped, madam moron. My whiskey's in the satchel. Bring it in."

Doreen's eyes soured for the briefest of seconds, but she didn't hold it long enough for Buster to notice. She did as he demanded and got him his whiskey. It was in a plastic bottle that had a faded label on it that read, 'Ketchup.'

He unscrewed the lid and took a swig. "I know'd your old man before he went off to the war."

"Yeah?"

"I was only a couple of years older than you are now at the time." He sipped from his bottle.

I didn't respond. I didn't care much about anything he had to say.

"He wasn't no hero when he left, if you want to know the truth. He really wasn't much more than a joke to most of us."

He got my ire up. "Like to hear you say that to his face."

He snickered. "He's broke all to hell, boy. I could put your old man down sooner than I could tie my shoe."

"Got my doubts you can tie your shoes. Besides, he's on the mend."

"No matter. He could be 110% of what he used to be, and he'd still be a joke."

"Don't nobody else think that."

"Everybody else thinks that. They just won't speak their mind 'cause Old Kelly owes your pa a debt."

"Debt?"

He looked at me with a mouth full of whiskey and swallowed. "Ain't your old man told you none of this?"

"He don't talk much about the way things were. He says there ain't no use."

Buster shook his head. "Peculiar. He, you're pa that is, saved Old Kelly's girl in the war. She got shot all the hell, and your pa drug her to safety or some nonsense like that. She come home with half her face blown off and missing both legs, but she come home. That was enough as far as Old Kelly was concerned. The platoon leader explained to Old Kelly what your pa had done, and the old bag ain't never forgot. That's why she lets you all keep to yourself on that property of yours. And that's why we ain't ate your horse. Hell, she even lets him skip worship."

"My pa done that?"

Buster nodded. "That's what they say. Don't make him more of man than me. I can tell you that right now."

"You go to war?"

"I did not," he said after sucking some whiskey down his gullet.

"Why not?"

"Never called on me. I got close. They send notice that my number come up, but that's the last I heard about it or the war or anything else outside of Two Notch. Everything just shut down."

"You think the war is still going on?"

"Can't say for sure. I got my doubts though."

"Why?"

"'Cause I'm pretty damn sure we ain't got a government no more. If we had, we'd be at war. That's just what governments do."

"Why you think we ain't got a government?"

"Well, we ain't got much in Two Notch, but we still got it. If the government was around, they'd find reason to come and take it. That's something else governments do."

"They don't sound all that appealing," I said.

He grunted when his bottle didn't produce anymore whiskey. "They're what you call necessary evils. We need 'em to make and keep the law. Individuals can't be trusted to nut up for that kind of work, or if they do, they're usually the wrong sort. Governments protect the weak from the strong and the strong from themselves."

"That don't make no sense."

"Of course it don't." He tossed his bottle aside. "Don't suppose you got any whiskey rations."

"Nope."

"Bet your pa don't even take his."

"He does, but he trades it for food and what not."

Buster shook his head in disgust. "That is just about the most depressing thing I have ever heard. What nots for whiskey? I'd sooner give up my right arm before my drink. If ever I needed a reason not to like your pa even more, that there tears it." He reached in his coat pocket and pulled out a pill bottle. "Guess I'll have to break into my mind altering provisions. Your pa get these?"

I shook my head. I'd heard Scooter Trundle talk up his daddy's pills. Says they drove his old man out of his head. Made him scarier than usual.

"Course not. Your pa's a regular boy scout."

"A what?"

"Boy scout. Something boys used to be before the war."

"Was you a boy scout?"

He looked at me cross. "How old do you think I am?"

"I don't know."

"I ain't never known a time before the war. I've just been told things about how it used to work." He fiddled with the cap on the bottle, but couldn't get it off.

"How'd it use to work?"

Doreen wandered over and sat next to me.

Buster looked up from his bottle with his tongue sticking out from the corner of his mouth. "Your pa ain't never said nothing to you about before?"

"Said something about football, but that's about it."

"Football? Yeah, I heard about that. They used to pay fellas to play that game."

"Really?"

He twisted the cap and still couldn't get it off. "You think I'm lying?"

"No, but maybe the fella that told you lied to you. Sounds silly to pay somebody for playing a game."

"My granddad told me. He was a cantankerous old shit, but he wasn't a liar." He groaned. "How in the hairy hell did folks used to take medicine if they locked up their drugs in these goddamn things?"

Doreen stood and reached out her hand.

Buster stared at her. "You think you can do better, simple girl?"

She didn't respond. She just kept her hand extended.

Buster snickered and stood. He flashed an ugly grin at me and then slapped the bottle down in Doreen's hand. "Here ya' go, shit-for-brains. I'll make a deal with you. You get that there cap off, and I'll give you a hunk of ham and biscuit from my feed bag. You fail and I get a little kiss from you."

I looked at him dumbfounded. "She's too young for something like that."

He flopped down on his flabby backside. "Says who?"

"Says Old Kelly's law. She had Clark Jefferson beat bloody with a leather strap for stealing a kiss from a girl two years older than Doreen last year."

"That was Jed Paulson's girl. Jed's a relation to Old Kelly. This one ain't. Plus she's barren so she don't come under the law."

I stood and took the bottle from Doreen. "I ain't going to let her agree to those conditions."

"You lifting up on me?" Buster asked. "I'll pound you to dust if you're lifting up on me."

"I ain't lifting up on you," I said. "You got me by a hundred and fifty pounds. I ain't stupid. Just don't think it's right, that's all. Doreen's a kid."

"And I told you before, I'm an A-dult. My say carries more weight. I say she ain't covered by Old Kelly's law."

Doreen quickly yanked the bottle from my hands and opened the bottle with little effort. Buster and me was so stunned we just stared at the open bottle. Eventually, I started to laugh.

"That's that," Buster said reaching for the bottle.

I pulled Doreen's hand out of his reach. "You said something about a hunk of ham and biscuit."

He flashed a wicked grin. "I did?"

"You did."

"Well, about that. I may have misspoke about my actual present possession of said ham."

I rolled my eyes. I have to say I wasn't completely surprised, but I was peeved all the same. "And the biscuit?"

"Got hardtack, but I can't hardly part with that."

"Why not?"

He stepped towards us. "'Cause I don't care to."

I took the open bottle of pills and held it over the fire, tilting it slightly so he could see my intentions to let his precious mind altering rations spill into the crackling flames.

"Hold on! Don't do that!"

"You made a promise of ham and biscuit to Doreen if she opened your bottle. She opened it. She deserves what you promised."

"I told you I ain't got no ham, but I'll give her some hardtack."

I studied the proposition. "What else you got?"

"Nothing."

I tilted the bottle a little more.

"Whoa! I got a bag of gopher nuts!"

"Cooked?"

"Roasted with a touch of cinnamon."

I looked at Doreen to get her approval on the deal. She raised an eyebrow and jerked her head to the left to indicate it didn't really matter to her. "That'll do."

"Fine. Hand over the pills."

"Now you must think I am some kind of stupid. Fetch the hardtack and gopher nuts, and I'll give over the bottle."

Buster hurried to his moped and pulled his pack free. He found the bag of gopher nuts before he reached us and was already digging through the contents to find the hardtack. "You ain't no kid, Henry Arnaught. You're a snake."

"I'm feeling less and less charitable, Buster Darnell." I tilted the bottle a tad more.

"Stop!" He pulled the paper bag from the pack. "Got it." He threw both small bags to Doreen.

"Okay," I said. "Now we got a bit of a problem."

"No we ain't. I give her the food like I said."

"Yeah, but you ain't in any kind of mood."

"I'll be right as rain if'n you give me my pills."

"You're just saying that because you want your pills."

"I ain't! I swear!"

"Don't worry. I got a solution." I kept my hand over the fire and turned to Doreen. "Bring me my daddy's army issue."

"You ain't got no cause to shoot me."

Doreen smiled and skipped to my stack of belongings. She bent down and awkwardly picked up the gun. She carried it with some difficulty and stood beside me.

"You remember what my Pa said… about the red and blue?"

She nodded.

"Point it at Buster and put your finger on the red trigger.

"There ain't no need for that…"

"Ain't nobody going to shoot you unless you give cause."

Doreen hoisted the gun up and rested the butt against her belly. She struggled mightily to aim it at Buster. When she had it in place, she closed one eye and placed her finger on the red trigger.

"Behave," I said to Buster

He held up his hands.

I held out the open bottle of pills. "Take it."

He started for it like a starving man going after a sandwich

"Slow!"

He stopped and then continued like he was swimming through syrup. He carefully took the bottle out of my hand and stepped back. "I swear I don't know what I done to get stuck with the likes of you two. I'd sooner hug a cactus than set my eyes on either one of you again once the sun comes up."

"Feeling's mutual."

He was about to tip some pills into his dirty hands when a howl came out of the canyon pass. He was visibly shaken. "Lord! If that don't set you on edge…"

Doreen wasn't as obvious about her dislike of the sound, but she moved subtly closer to me.

"What was that?" I asked trying to be even more subtle than Doreen about the state of my frayed nerves.

"Nothing good." He dumped two pills in the palm of his hand.

"You sure you want to do that?" I motioned toward the canyon. "Might should be on your toes in case of any incidental events."

He popped the pills in his mouth and swallowed. "Got no interest in dealing with incidental events. We got nothing to worry about. They never leave the pass, far as I know."

"What are they?"

"Sheer terror is what they are. I never seen nothing more than their eyes. Big green eyes."

"Green?"

"Glowed like lanterns."

"I ain't never heard of an animal with lantern eyes."

"Who says they're animals?"

I looked at him like he was the most peculiar creature on the planet. "What are you saying?"

He giggled. I couldn't tell if the drugs was getting to him or if he was playing a joke on us. "I'm saying they might be people. Ain't nobody ever come back with a clear description of them. Anybody who's been close enough to say what they are…" His eyes looked like they were floating in their sockets.

"What?"

He blinked and shook his head like a wet dog. "World looks a bit pale."

"What happened to folks who got a good look at the lantern eyes?"

"Don't know. Them folks ain't never been seen again."

I felt something squeezing my forearm. I looked down and saw that Doreen had a white-knuckled grip on me. "How'd you see their eyes?"

"Got caught in the pass at dark." He leaned back and let out a loud "Ha!" He beat his chest. "That ain't an enviable position to be in, boy Arnaught."

"My Pa says it ain't sensible."

"Now, if that ain't the most unnecessary thing ever spoken." He laughed and a little drool came out of his mouth.

"He don't like to leave nothing unsaid when it comes to living cautiously."

"He raised you like you was an egg that might crack at any moment."

"That's your opinion."

"That's the opinion of every-damn-body, boy Arnaught."

"Says you."

"You lifting up on me again?"

I shook my head. "I ain't."

He jerked forward and put his hand over his mouth. It appeared as if he was about to puke all over the place, but he held it in and sat back up. "I'll tell you something though. Unnecessary or not, your Pa is right on the button about getting caught in the pass at dark. It ain't sensible. Far from it."

"How'd you get caught?"

"Well, if you time it right, you can make it from one end to other while the sun's out. Take out at the right exact time and you'll never see a shade of darkness in the pass, 'cept for a small bit at the other end. Miscalculate and your goose is cooked."

"You miscalculated?"

"Yeah." His head started to wobble. He held up his hand with his thumb and pointing finger separated by the smallest space. "But just by a hair. Me and Donald Payne got fifty feet from the end of the pass when we heard a howl, 'bout the same as we caught wind of a minute or two ago."

"I don't know no Donald Payne."

Buster burst out laughing at first, but it quickly turned into a horrible fit of sobbing.

It was a spectacle. I turned to Doreen and whispered, "He's gone drug crazy."

"You don't know Donald Payne 'cause he didn't make it out of the pass. The lantern eyes got 'em. We was neck and neck sprinting to get clear of the canyon. We was scared, but we was also a bit excited by the thrill of it. Your blood pumps a little faster, and you feel like you can run out of your skin."

"They got Donald?"

"Yanked him off his feet. I couldn't see nothing. It was like they were ghosts. I guess they were distracted by him to give me time enough to break through the pass."

"You never saw nothing?"

"Nothing. Heard' em. Snorting and growling. Sounded like their jaws was snapping shut."

I leaned in closer to Doreen. The thought of them things prowling the canyon no more than 20 or 30 yards from where I was sitting was getting more and more unsettling. I felt the hair stand up on the back of my neck and a chill went through me.

"They're heavy whatever they are. I could hear their feet hit the ground. Sounded like a herd of them." He snorted. Something funny occurred to him, but he never shared it with us. He pointed at the army issue that Doreen had propped up next to her. "That thing probably won't do nothing but piss 'em off."

"Can't see how that could be."

"Can't kill demons with guns."

"Demons?"

"That's what I said."

"But I thought you said you didn't see them."

"Don't have to see a demon to know a thing is a demon." He stood and walked toward the head of the pass.

Doreen tugged on my arm.

"Where you going?"

"I got something I want to say to them."

"That ain't a good idea."

"Relax," he said as he stumbled, almost falling to his knees He righted himself and kept walking. "I ain't going in." His walk turned into a shuffle as he got as close to the pass as he could without stepping into it. "Hey, demons! You remember me? You took my friend Donald Payne, you sons-a-bitches! I hope you choked on his bones!" He turned to us and flashed a goofy grin. Back to the canyon he said, "I ain't afraid of you!"

Another howl shot out of the canyon.

Buster screamed and fell ass-first to the ground.

Doreen covered her mouth as she giggled madly. I waited for the demons to yank Buster into the pass, but they never came. He slid a few feet back and then just flopped flat on his back on the ground.

"This here's a good place to sleep."

***

I ain't got the first idea how, but I slept like a baby that night. An earthquake would have had a time rousing me. I stretched and yawned and took a second or two to soak in my restfulness. It was a feeling that was a godsend not only in our times, but also considering the day I had ahead of me.

I stood and noticed the fire had gone down to its embers. It didn't give off but the smallest amount of heat. The sun was just peeking through, so it was still nippy. I stuck my hands as close to the smoldering wood chunks as I could without actually sticking my hand in the ash. It had not occurred to me that I was alone. That hit me when my stomach was rumbling. I turned to Doreen's bedroll to ask what she wanted for breakfast, but she wasn't there. I whirled around to where Buster had passed out, and he wasn't there either. Runner whinnied and I jerked my head around in his direction. There sitting on my father's saddle was that no-good Buster Darnell aiming my father's army issue at me.

"Got to thinking," he said. "Old Kelly probably ain't got odds on you coming back. Kind of a waste of a horse and a gun."

"So, you gonna kill me?"

"That's more or less the point."

"Pa will rip you to shreds."

He laughed. "That broken down old piece of shit couldn't rip a page out of a book."

"You go ahead and count on that. Pa could put you down if he was half of what he is now, Buster Darnell."

He laughed even harder. "Boy Arnaught, you got a thing or two to learn about your daddy and you ain't got much time to learn it. I'll cut to the quick. He's a coward. Run from more fights than he stood his ground. Broke his back doing just that."

"That ain't true."

He leaned forward. "It's true if I say it is. You know why?"

I shook my head.

"Cause I got the gun. Them's the rules. The guy with the gun gets to tell the stories." He aimed at me.

"You ride into town on my mount and Old Kelly will know you stole him and killed me."

"Thought of that. I'm going to butcher him for meat at Peter Deet's place. He'll keep his mouth shut for a portion of the meat."

I gritted my teeth. "You're a low down pot of shit!"

He grinned. "Them your last words?"

I looked around. "Where's Doreen? What'd you do with her?"

"She was gone when I woke. She's probably snaking through the pass as we speak. It's a fool's move, but what do you expect from a simple girl." He tightened his grip on the army issue and prepared to pull the trigger. "I best be on my way."

"I'm going to haunt you, Buster. Every night of the rest of your life, I'm going to make your life a living hell."

"You'll have to get in line, kid 'cause I got plenty of ghosts haunting me…"

A rock struck him in the temple and he stiffened like a corpse. He was on the ground before I could catch my breath.

Doreen stepped out from behind a row of brush. She had another rock cocked and ready to throw.

"Pegged him," I said approaching Buster slowly. "Still don't know how you do that, but I'm pleased as pleased can be that it's one of your talents."

She smiled widely.

I moved around Runner and examined Buster. He had a red welt forming on the side of his head where the rock had hit him. His eyes were shut, and he still had a loose grip on my Pa's army issue. His chest was moving up and down. "He ain't dead," I said.

She walked over tossing the other rock in the air.

"You already knew that, didn't you?"

She just kept tossing the rock and grinning like a fiend.

"We better get him tied up before he comes to. Fetch me his supplies."

She dropped the rock and ran to Runner to get Buster's backpack. I pulled the gun out of his hands and went through his pockets. I didn't find nothing but his bottle of pills and an unsettling amount of dirt and grime. I was wiping my hands on his shirttail when Doreen handed me his pack. I rifled through it and found a knife and spare shirt that was as filthy as the one he was wearing. I cut it up into strips and rolled him over. Pa had taught me knot tying when I was young, but it never really came in handy until now. Buster was bound like a pig on a spit.

I kept going through his back and groaned when I found a hunk of ham wrapped in aluminum foil. "Son-of-a-bitch lied." I held up the ham, "You earned this," I said to Doreen.

She took it from me and smelled it.

"It ain't bad. Been cured with salt for keeping."

She tore off a piece and handed the rest to me. I didn't argue with her. If she wanted to share, who was I to disagree? I tore off a piece for myself and took to chewing the tough as leather meat. It was salty enough to make my eyes water. "Can't hardly see the use in salting it this much."

She nodded with her eyes almost squinted shut.

I took one more bite and then shoved the rest in my pocket. "It ain't much of a meal, but it'll do in a pinch. I'll just wait for the pinch."

She nodded and put the rest of what she had in her coat pocket.

Buster didn't have much more in the way of provisions. He had a bit of water, and I had every right to take it, but I couldn't bring myself to do it. He was going to have a hard enough time wriggling out of the knots I set. He was set on killing me, and he said some awful lies about my Pa, but I didn't much care for killing no one, not even Buster Darnell.

I holstered the gun and helped Doreen up on Runner. I was about to mount when I heard Buster stir.

"What the hell?" he asked as he lifted his head and spit out some dirt. He squirmed and kicked and let out a yelp of pain.

"You're all right," I said squatting down beside him.

"How'd you get the drop on me, boy?"

"Didn't. She did." I pointed up at Doreen who was sitting on Runner with a proud smile spread across her face. "Pretty good for a simple girl, huh?"

He jerked his hands about behind his back. "Got me in a fix, do ya?"

"Best I could. You'll work your way free 'fore long."

"You ain't gonna kill me?"

"My Pa taught me to be charitable when it comes to matters of life and death."

"He's a good man, you're Pa."

"Really? That's not what you said before."

He worked with all his might to roll over. "That was the pills talking. That whole thing I done, the talk of killing you and stealing your horse and saying them things about your Pa, that was just me out of my mind from the drugs."

I reached in my pocket and pulled out the pills. "These drugs?"

"Whatcha got my pills for?"

"Might come in handy for trades along the way."

"You're going to leave me tied up here without provisions or pills or nothing?"

"I left you some water in your pack. 'Course you gotta work yourself free to get at it."

He tugged on his binding. "You got me confined pretty tight. Take me all day to work out of these."

I stood. "That's a possibility, but I'm willing to take that chance." I climbed on Runner's back.

"Wait! I can go with you. Show you the way. Save you some peril."

"You ain't done nothing but add to our peril since we left Two Notch, Buster Darnell."

"I'll turn around right. I swear. You need me."

"Old Kelly says once we get through the pass we'll find Abel Decker if we head East. Don't need you for that." I steered Runner toward the head of the pass.

"Wait!" Buster shouted. "You're leaving too late! Darkness will fall on you in the canyon! You gotta wait until tomorrow!"

I didn't listen to him. I was certain he was just trying to scare us into staying with him.

"I ain't lying! Them lantern eyes will get hold of you before you're half a mile from the pass."

I stopped and looked over my shoulder at him. "I'd rather tangle with the lantern eyes than spend another minute with you."

"That's tough talk that'll do you in, Henry Arnaught. You'll get that girl killed, too. Ain't no question about it."

I urged Runner on and we entered the pass.

6

It felt like Besser canyon was swallowing us. Runner ambled along the dry riverbed and the rust colored canyon walls stretched to the sky on both sides of us. I popped my head from left to right and took in as much of it as I could. It was beautiful in a scare-the-living-hell out of ya' kind of way. Mostly it just felt like the world was shrinking before your very eyes.

We rounded a bend and Doreen tapped my shoulder. She pointed to an outcropping of rocks just ahead. They looked like they were moving. I narrowed my eyes and tried to make out how such a thing could be. It was water moving down the face of the rock.

"Lordy." I kicked Runner, and he bounded toward the water, flaring his nostrils, catching wind of the smell of water. He slowed and then stopped a few feet from the rock. I followed the trail of the water all the way to the top of the cliff. "It's just falling down the rock." Runner stretched his neck out and started lapping up the water.

"I ain't never seen nothing like it. How do you reckon it does that?"

Of course, Doreen didn't answer.

I stuck my hand out and cupped it underneath a small ledge. The water was just coming off it in drips, but it was enough to soak my palm quick as a hiccup. I licked my hand. "Tastes a little rusty."

Doreen leaned out and did the same.

I unwrapped the canteen from around the saddle horn and opened it. "If we collect enough, Old Kelly can't say nothing about sharing my water rations with you. We might even get that gold she talked about." I stuck the canteen under the ledge and let the water drip into it.

I felt it necessary to fill the quiet with chatter. "That Buster's one for stories, huh? Going on about things with lantern eyes and making up some poor fella who got carried off by them. Even trying to tell us we let out too late. He enjoys scaring folks, is what it is. Especially kids. He thinks he put one over on us. Thinks we's idiots, scared little rug rats that get rattled by silly stories." I forced out a laugh.

She reached out a few times and scooped up her fill of the rock water.

"You don't reckon we left too late, do ya'?"

She didn't acknowledge my question.

"S'pose it ain't the wisest thing to just sit still like this when daylight is burning." I pulled the canteen back and put the lid back on. "'Spect there's more of this falling water deeper in the pass." I tugged on the reins and moved Runner out onto the riverbed. He wasn't happy in the least about giving up the water.

I spurred him with a gentle jab to the ribs, so he'd pick up the pace. He tried to bite me on one occasion, but I seen him turning his head with that look in his eyes, and I was able to avoid the chomp on my leg. He snorted at being bested and reluctantly trotted farther into the canyon.

The canyon was considerably cooler than the open sky between Two Notch and the head of the pass. The wind flickered and fluttered about, providing a cool breeze every step of the way. Coats was a necessity. Doreen pulled in and hugged me tight to keep herself warm. Normally, I would have complained, but truth be known, it kept me a great deal warmer, too.

"You want to hear a story?" I asked. "It's about the only way I know to pass the time."

She squeezed me tighter and I took that as a yes.

"'Bout two-years ago me, and Billy Robbins was milling around downtown Two Notch. We were looking in the windows of some of the abandon buildings. Ain't nothing but dust and dirt in most of them. We was popping from broken window front to broken window front peeking inside, trying to imagine what in the hell they used to be. Pa says he can remember a time when every one of them was filled with people, some was getting their hairs cut. Some was buying coffee drinks. Ladies was buying shoes. Men was drinking beer and complaining about their women buying too many shoes. Pa said if you could sell it, eat it, drink it or bitch about it, they had a shop for it in downtown Two Notch.

"Anyway, like I said, me and Billy was running from window to window and we wasn't seeing much of nothing. I was getting bored with the activity if you want to know the truth. I was just about to suggest we pass our time another way when, wouldn't you know it, Billy called out, 'Lookie here, Henry.'

"He was peering in the window of a place my Pa said they called McDonalds. He says it was a place where people used to get fat as pig studs. You heard of the place?"

She propped her chin into my back and shook her head so I could feel it.

"They sold something called fast food. S'pose it was a place where you had to catch your food. Which don't make any kind of sense. If people is chasing after critters to eat, that sounds like a good deal of exercising, don't it? How'd they get so fat?"

I felt her shrug.

"Anyway, I peeked into the window to see what had Billy all worked up, and there on a counter was this box, 'bout a quarter the size of your average tackle box. Right on the side there it said, 'Happy Meal.'

"Now, me and Billy held a discussion on what that could mean. What in the hell was a Happy Meal? That breakfast you and me had the other morning before we took off, that meal was pleasing, but I can't say it made me happy. I can't say I've ever had a meal that made me happy. I've felt relieved before. I've been grateful. Now, I may have been happy a meal that my Pa served up didn't kill me or make me puke my guts out, but nothing I've ever ate in my life made me happy. That must have been some kind of food in that box if it made you happy."

If Doreen had any kind of thoughts on the matter, she didn't break her silence over it.

"The world sounds like it used to be a paradise. If they had a place where you could get your fill of food and boxed meals that made you happy, what do you suppose got everybody all riled up and in the mood for a war? You'd think they wouldn't want to mess a thing like that up.

"Best I can figure is the war got going because someone wanted what someone else had. So much so that they killed a fella for it. That fella's people killed the other fella's people in reply. And it went on like that until that first fella's government got fed up and just sent in its army to set things right, but when they got there, they come up against the killing-fella's government soldiers. Pretty soon everyone was taking sides and mouthing off and hell took over.

"That's best I can figure anyway."

I heard her yawn.

"Pa said the war started near seventy-five years ago. I can't hardly conceive that many years. I don't even know a person that old. You?"

She shook her head.

"Old Kelly might be close. She looks like she's a thousand years old... don't tell her I said that... forgot you don't talk no way.

"Here's my question. If there ain't no one around who was here when the war started, why in the hell are they still going at it? I mean if they even are. As dumb as he is, Buster made good sense on that topic. Ain't no one from the government been around for years. Near ten according to my Pa. I reckon the war could be over and word just ain't got to Two Notch yet."

I felt her shrug again.

"Maybe Abel Decker's got some thoughts on it."

She laid her head against my back. I imagine she was about to drift off.

"You scared of meeting up with Decker?"

She yawned.

"I'll take that as a no. Tell ya' the truth, I'm feeling a bit skittish over it. Heard he's done awful things to friend and foe alike. All comes down to pay for a fella like that. That's where his loyalties sit. Pa said he used to have a partner, but he cut his throat one night under the stars. Don't nobody really know why, but there's all kind of speculation. Some say his partner tried to cheat him out of pay. Some say they got drunk and took to arguing about this and that. One thing led to another and Decker ran a blade across his neck. Billy says Decker killed his partner for snoring too loud. Can't believe a fella would do that, not even one as mean as Abel Decker."

Her grip around my waste loosened. Didn't take a brain doctor to know she was asleep.

"Sure wish you talked."

***

The dry riverbed snaked around a corner and dipped down a good bit. Runner had a tough time negotiating the rocky path. He fussed and stepped and fussed and stepped until we got back on flat ground. If Doreen woke during the descent, she didn't let on.

I steered Runner around a pile of rocks and debris. He fought every bit of the way. Came close to rearing up on at least one occasion, but he kept all fours on the hard surface. If I hadn't been tired out of my mind, I would've noticed that he was giving me signals. He was spooked about something. I didn't know what until we got around the pile of debris.

There was an assortment of bones scattered across the right side of the pass. Must have been the remains of dozens of animals. They were stripped clean and speckled with teeth marks. Most of it was livestock of some sort, which was surprising because I ain't never seen that many farm animals in one spot. The whole town of Two Notch hadn't had this many animals within the city limits since I've been alive.

I woke Doreen up and jumped off my mount. She wiped her eyes and stayed on top of Runner.

Bending down, I picked up a rib bone and examined the teeth marks. I'd been hunting with Pa enough to know my way around most animals in these parts. We come across stray bones here and there and he taught me what part of the animal they were, and to look for signs of predators. He claimed to know what animals were what by the teeth marks they left on the bone. I didn't pick up that knowledge, but I could tell whatever it was had pointed teeth. I tossed the rib and shuffled through a pile of fragmented bones until I come to a jaw bone. It gave me a start. It wasn't like no other jaw bone I'd ever seen before in my life. I picked it up and held it up to show Doreen. "What kind of animal you reckon this is?"

Her eyes got wide and she sat up straight.

"What?"

She rubbed the side of her face from her seat on the back of Runner.

"Something wrong with your jaw…?" My eyes widened cause I knew what she was trying to tell me. "It's a person?"

She nodded.

I dropped the bone and wiped my hands on my pants in a fit. "I reckon that might be one Donald Payne," I said doing my best to climb up on the saddle. Runner whinnied and stepped to the side. I had hold of the saddle horn, but I was slipping. Doreen grabbed onto one of my belt loops and pulled with all her strength. I repositioned myself and accidentally knee'd runner in the ribs. He jumped forward and took off like a shot. I come close to losing my grip.

"Let up, Runner!" I shouted and it echoed through the canyon. "I can't hold on, you dumb shit horse!"

Doreen leaned forward and grabbed the reins. She pulled back and Runner stopped but not without raising up on his hind legs and huffing up in madness.

I let go of the saddle horn and dropped ass-first to the ground. I sat up and let out a grunt. "Shit if that weren't good-goddamned unnecessary!" The sound of snickering caught my ear.

Doreen had a hand over her mouth. She was quivering with laughter.

I held back a smile and stood up. "It's funny cause neither one of us got hurt. But if things had gone the wrong way, if we'd broke a bone or bashed our heads, we'd be stuck in this canyon for the night."

She stopped laughing.

"The state of them bones back there makes me take more stock of Buster's lantern eyes story." I mounted Runner without incident. "I don't know if they got eyes like he says, but I tell you one thing I know for sure about whatever done that to them animals... and that person back there. Whatever it was has got teeth. Teeth I ain't got much interest in seeing up close."

***

I pushed Runner as fast as he could go for the next mile. He didn't argue too much. He would have given me more for a lot longer, but he didn't have but a drop of water left in him and he was hungry. I didn't want to, but I stopped at the widest spot in the riverbed and announced that Runner needed a rest.

I instructed Doreen to give him some of our water rations while I explored the left side of the bed for even the smallest amount of vegetation, anything that Runner could eat and give us his mount just until we were clear of the canyon.

The ghost of the riverbank was thirty feet from Doreen and Runner. A series of rock piles hid the cliff face from view, and I was hesitant to investigate what was on the other side of the piles given what we found behind the last pile of debris. I tried hard to convince myself that it wasn't necessary. Runner could go on with just a couple of hands full of water, couldn't he? I sneaked a peek at him to gauge his overall fitness. His head was hung low, and he was licking his lips. Doreen was stroking his neck. He was tuckered out. It was plain as day. I sucked it up and climbed the smallest pile of rocks to the top. It gave me enough height to stretch over the next tallest pile and see what was on the other side. To my utter amazement, there was about a ten foot by ten foot patch of waist high green grass. I'd seen about twenty strands of green grass in my entire life, and there I was staring at a whole uninterrupted chunk of grass.

I pushed back and looked for a way to get Runner around the rock piles so he could feed, but there was no entrance big enough for him. There wasn't an entrance big enough for me. I'd have to keep climbing and jump down the other side and snatch up some grass for him. If I'd been thinking straight, I'd thought better of that idea. Them rocks didn't get there on their own. Somebody or something put them there. It was a wall.

But I wasn't thinking straight, so I climbed from the smaller pile to the bigger pile and dropped down on the other side. It was a good twelve foot drop, but it didn't bother me none. Pa thought I was born with springs in my knees to take the falls I had in my life.

I grabbed the grass as far down the stalk as I could and pulled. It didn't budge. I reworked my grip and pulled until my shoulder muscles burned and my head felt like it was going to pop. I stood, took a deep breath, and told myself there was no way in hell grass was going to get the best of me. I reached down and grabbed on again. Counting one, two, three I jerked back quick. The grass tore loose from the ground, and I went flying backwards into the face of the cliff. When I hit, I felt something give away. Still holding onto the grass, I turned to where I struck the cliff and noticed a crack. Had I broke the cliff? Was that possible? I examined the crack and noticed that it was surrounded by a different material than the rest of the rock face. It was almost like dry clay. The more I dug at it with my finger, the more of it give way. I picked up a nearby stick and ran it along the crack. I did that several times, each time applying more and more pressure until at one point the stick busted through, creating a hole.

"This is craziness," I said peeking into the hole. It didn't do no good because it was pitch black. I took a closer look and discovered a large round area, 'bout big enough for a man to pass through, that was a slightly different color than the rocks that made up the cliff. I had poked through a clay seal of some kind. I had never heard of such a thing. It was out of place enough to unsettle my nerves a great deal. I returned to plucking up grass. I stuffed it in my pockets and shirt and up my pants leg quick as I could. Once I stuffed as much grass as I could on my person, I scrambled to find a foothold, so I could climb back over the rock piles. It was tough sledding. There wasn't much to get my purchase on this side of the piles, but after enough time and searching, I made my way to the top of the rocks. I scooted on my belly over the top and hoisted my legs over. Taking a minute to catch my breath, I peered back down at the hole I had created with the stick and nearly flung myself backwards when I seen an eye looking back at me. I scurried down the rocks without much thought of injury. An eye looking out of a hole in a rock wall will do wonders for your tolerance of such minor inconveniences.

My feet hit the dry bank in motion. I was half way to Runner and Doreen before I knew I was even on the ground. "Mount up!" I yelled. "Mount up!"

Doreen looked at me with a great deal of concern on her face. If she was one to talk, she would have asked what had me on edge, but thankfully, talking was not in her nature. Now, she didn't climb onto Runner's back, of course. She wasn't big enough to mount him on her own. In my haste to escape the eye of the cliff, that memory had slipped my mind. I headed for her, pissed as hell that she wasn't taking my pleas seriously.

"Get on Runner!"

She turned and attempted to but she couldn't jump high enough to reach the top of the saddle. Watching her do her best to climb up on Runner was all the trigger I needed to remember that she couldn't do it on her own. Hell, I could barely do it on my own. I reached her and hoisted her up on Runner, and in less than two shakes I was sitting in Runner's saddle. "Let's get up and go, boy. This ain't no time to lollygag."

***

Runner done the best he could on the fuel he had left in his belly. We put about a quarter of a mile between us and the... whatever it was I seen. I dismounted and did what I could to settle my nerves. I was breathing like someone was stepping on my lungs.

Doreen gave me a curious look.

"I seen..." I bent over and placed my hands on my knees. I was itching like the devil. "I seen this thing..." I took to scratching and was confused when I couldn't feel my own fingers racking across my chest. I saw the grass sticking out of my shirt around my wrist and caught on. I was stuffed full of the itchy stuff. I yanked out a handful from the top of my shirt and fed it to Runner. I dislodged the rest and threw it on the ground while I tried to give a good account of what I seen. "There was a cave or something back there. Somebody sealed up the entrance with clay. Fresh from what I could tell. Brittle, but kind of damp, like it was just set to drying."

She crossed her arms and smirked like I was some sort of fool.

"I ain't out of my head on this. I swear I seen it. I poked a stick right through it. Seen..." I didn't want to give her any more cause to think I was bat-shit crazy. "I seen something else, too."

She tapped her finger against her arm and gave me the cock-eye.

"I'll tell you, but don't make no judgment on me. I seen what I seen. I can't help it."

She shrugged.

"I seen an eye."

She rolled her eyes.

"I said don't make no judgment. I seen an eye looking right through that hole I poked. I swear it. It wasn't green, like Buster said."

Runner was busy chomping on a mouthful of grass, but even he took the time to look at me like I'd lost my senses.

"Fine, don't believe me. Either one of ya', but I can promise you this. I ain't going nowhere without my Pa's army issue anymore." I examined the sky. The sun had moved down over the top of the cliff. "We ain't got but a couple of hours before night time's on us." I watched Runner bend his head down for more grass. He seemed to be taking his sweet time.

Doreen jumped off his back.

"What are you doing? We can't be wasting time. Once he's had his fill, we need to get out of here as fast as his hooves can carry us."

She didn't pay no attention to me. Just turned and walked toward a bend in the canyon. I started to follow but she put out her hand to stop me. "My Pa said we shouldn't let the other out of our sight. I went over them rocks back there where you couldn't see me, and I paid for it with a big frightful eye looking at me through the canyon wall."

She stared at me with her hand still up.

"It ain't a good idea. He said even if you was doing your business I should keep an eye on you."

She tilted her head to the side and smiled.

"Oh, I get it. You're off to do your business."

She nodded and turned.

I stepped in her direction and stopped. My desire not to see such a thing as her evacuating trumped my call to duty to keep an eye on her. Daylight was on us. She was safe.

So there I stood listening to Runner chew itchy grass and waiting for Doreen to come back around the bend. It was an intolerable wait. She was a little thing that barely had any food or water in her system. You wouldn't think it would take her so long to purge herself.

I waited and waited and waited, but she never appeared. Runner was down to his last bit of grass, and I begun to mumble under my breath about what a goddamn inconvenience it was to have to keep up with a baby that can't hold her bladder long enough for us to cut through the pass.

"Rock throwing talents aside, Runner, that girl draws a pain in my gut. She's just another damn thing to worry about."

He snorted.

I went for the gun and pulled it out of its saddle holster and then grabbed Runner's reins. "Look here. I can't fire a good shot mounted. Can barely do it with my feet on the ground. You got to promise me you won't take off running if we come across some trouble around that turn ahead."

He didn't acknowledge that he understood. That's the thing about horses. They can't talk, and they listening for shit.

I pulled him up the riverbed with my Pa's army issue draped over my shoulder. As we rounded the turn, I craned my neck to try and spot Doreen. She wasn't in sight. I let go of Runner's reins and held the gun at the ready at my waist. "Doreen, you still doing your business?"

She didn't answer. That's the thing about mutes. They're an awful lot like horses.

I moved into the area slowly, reaching the first rock outcropping with sweaty palms. I heard a scraping, as if a foot slipped from its hold above. I zipped my head in its direction and saw Doreen twenty feet up on the rocks. She was climbing with surprising ease.

"Whatcha doing wasting time climbing?"

She didn't acknowledge me.

"This is foolish when we got eyes looking through holes at us."

She reached a small ledge and reached for something that I couldn't see from my position. When she brought her hand back into sight, it had hold of a canvas bag.

"What is it?"

She opened the bag and looked inside. A smile crept across her face.

"What?"

She reached in the bag and pulled out a small yellow apple.

***

There were six apples in the bag, six glorious yellow apples. I proposed that we divide them up evenly even though she was the one who had discovered them and done all the climbing. She agreed, two for her, two for me and two for Runner.

I was growing more and more nerve-bitten at the prospect of not making it through the pass by sundown, so I decided that Runner would not get his first apple until we were safely out of the shadows of the canyon. That didn't prevent me and Doreen from tearing into our first apple en route. Runner looked back at us on a couple of occasions once he got a whiff of what we was eating. Can't say if he'd ever had a taste of an apple or not, but he liked the aroma. He appeared curious and resentful all at once. No amount of me reassuring him he'd get his in due time seemed to change his mood.

With a mouthful of apple, I said, "Who you reckon would go and leave a bag of apples in the middle of nowhere like that?"

I heard her bite into the firm fruit and break the skin. I imagined the juices was running down her chin.

"I ain't never seen so many at one time. Pa brought home two before. They were a lot smaller than these, and sour enough to seal your eyes shut for a day or two. These is about as sweet a thing as I have ever eaten."

I heard her suck up some of the juice.

"I'll be honest. I'm stuck on this being some kind of divine intervention, a present from the Lord above. Pa would say that's foolishness. He don't believe in that sort of thing. He'd say that it was just a stroke of good luck."

She tore loose a chunk of apple and chewed like a dog ripping meat from a bone.

"He'd say to me, 'Henry, in this world a man will find himself surrounded by unfortunate misfortunes and grasp at godly ways to break himself free. His belief in his worthiness of God is 100% dependent on the vein of luck running through any particular day'"

She swallowed and took another bite.

"I don't mind telling you my Pa has some depressing ways about him. Most my friends and their families pray at the drop of a hat. They pray for food. They pray when they get the food. They pray when they eat the food. They pray when it's sitting in they bellies. Hell, some of 'em even pray when they shit it out."

Runner shot me a look again.

I ignored him. "That's a bit on the excessive side. If I was God, last thing I'd want to do is talk to a fella while he's going to the toilet. Seems kind of rude, but if you're everywhere all the time, you're bound to see things you'd rather not anyhow. The conversation might distract you from the more unpleasant matters."

The riverbed became too rocky for Runner to navigate safely, so I steered him to the left bank, and we continued our trek on a smoother surface.

"Your people believe in God?"

She didn't answer. Not that I could tell anyway.

"What about you, you believe in God?" I said as I turned toward her.

She shrugged.

"That's 'bout the way I feel. Hard to say on a thing like that. My Ma did. Least that's what Pa says. She prayed a good bit, but nothing extreme. She done what Old Kelly mandated and a time or two more throughout the day."

I sniffed my apple and closed my eyes, soaking in the dreamy fragrance. "That's one thing that's got me leaning against the idea of God. Old Kelly. A more objectionable woman you will not meet. Why he'd lay his wisdom on her, just don't make no sense to me."

We come upon some writing on the rock wall. "Last bend Eastbound. No more salvation from the sun."

I nearly dropped my apple. "What in the tarnation do you reckon that means?"

Doreen had stopped chewing on her apple.

I had my answer when we rounded the bend. The cliffs towered higher on both sides and they connected at the top to make a land bridge. A dark stretch of the pass set out before us that was near 300 feet long.

"I ain't too keen on going through there," I said darting my head around in every direction looking for a path that would carry us up to the top of the cliff. I would have gladly added time to our trip by going up and then down once we got past the land bridge if it meant we didn't have to go through the piece of land that was dark as dark can be. There was no such path.

"But, on the other hand, once we clear it, it looks like we've made it through the pass."

Doreen did not offer up an opinion one way or the other, not that I expected her to.

I pulled Pa's army issue from its holster and laid it across the saddle in front of me. "Red is for ammo. Blue is for pulse," I said with some hesitation. My present state of fear played tricks on my thinking, and I was not confident in my recall of Pa's instructions.

I goaded Runner into a trot and off we went into the tunnel of doom. Ten feet in and I was struck by an immediate and painful sense of regret. Not just at our present position, but at my unfortunate misfortunes that set me on this trip in the first plate. It occurred to me that if we had made a meal out of Runner some time ago, I would not be entering the throat of the miserable darkness I was now entering.

"I reckon it's times like these where people call up on prayers."

I patted Runner on the neck, and he turned his head to me. Reaching in the canvas sack Doreen had found, I fumbled for the biggest apple my hands could get a hold of and pulled it out. "You see this here apple, Runner. You get us through this tunnel fast as the wind, and I'll let you have it."

He whinnied and grunted, and dug his front right hoof into the dirt. I took that to meaning he understood. I felt his muscles tense. "Smack him on the behind, Doreen, and then hold on. If I know Runner, he'll rear up and then beat the ground with his hooves at a hundred miles an hour."

Doreen gripped me tight around the waist and then gave old Runner a good slap on the rump.

Bam! Runner raised up and leapt forward. He tore across the cracked riverbed like his very life depended on it.

The second the dark hit us I heard an excitement from all around us. There was some kind of babbling and squeals coming from the ledges that lined both sides of the rock walls, but nothing popped out of the shadows and showed their faces. If I didn't know no better, I'd swear they were passing word down the line that we was coming.

Doreen had both arms wrapped around me now. She was squeezing the life out of me, and she had her head pasted against my back. I could feel hot breath coming in quick, excitable spurts.

The farther into the tunnel we got, the clearer the exit became. It was the very end of the pass. We had a hundred yards ahead of us, and then we was beyond the haunts of Besser Canyon.

I turned to let Doreen know we was almost there when I seen a man or something that stood on two legs anyhow, step out from behind a big rock on the left bank. I swear to the God my Pa don't believe in that he had green glowing eyes – lantern eyes.

I kicked Runner over and over again. A good panic had set in from my bones on out. "Faster! C'mon, Runner! Faster!"

We was ten feet from the opening. That was it. I could smell the dry open air of freedom. It was a glorious odor that I ain't never appreciated before. I was about to let myself relax when I heard a snap. The awful noise was followed by Runner tumbling to the ground, tossing me and Doreen out past the darkness of the tunnel.

I wriggled in pain for a second or two. I was confused by the whole event. I couldn't get my bearings on what took place. I managed to sit up. The back of my head had taken a good thumping. I rubbed it and surveyed the area blurry-eyed. "Doreen," I said.

I heard a groan to my left and watched as the little simple girl who could throw a rock like nobody's business stood up. She was scraped here and there, but she looked otherwise fine.

A horrible high-pitched whinny come from behind me. I turned to see Runner on the ground. His snout was in the light, but the rest of him lay in the darkness. I stood and wobbled over to him. He was in a terrible load of pain. It didn't take long for me to figure out why. One of his front legs was broke clean through. I couldn't move a muscle looking at it. All sorts of thoughts fired off in my head.

I had failed my Pa. I was sent on this trip because he didn't trust no one else with his pony. Fat tub of good that did him now. His horse was mangled with the only person he trusted looking after it.

I near killed Doreen and me pushing Runner to go faster just 'cause I got scared. If there was ever any question about it before, there wasn't now. I wasn't no kind of man. Not in the least little bit.

And worst of all, I kept on thinking about how poor old Runner was suffering so. He was in a frightful amount of pain. Pa said there was only one way to deal with a horse with a broken leg.

That's when another thought come to me, Pa's army issue.

"We's on foot from here," I said.

Doreen stepped up and stood next to me. She didn't whimper or blubber like a baby looking at Runner, but I seen a tear drip from the corner of her eye.

A howl, the same howl we heard the night before from the other side of the pass, rose up out of the darkness. Followed by another and then another.

"They're excited about something," I said. I knew what that something was, but I couldn't bring myself to say. They had a horse meal waiting on the pass for them.

It took a second or two to work up a fair amount of courage, and then I took a step into the darkness. The howling got more intense. I bit my lower lip and took another step. The howling was joined by a shitful of screeches and squawks. They were probably in the mind now that they had two meals on the pass.

I bent down and worked Pa's army issue free from underneath Runner. It felt heavier than it ever had before. Probably 'cause there was no question this time. I was going to have to pull the red trigger.

I put the butt of the gun against my shoulder and heard Pa's firing instructions in my head. Doreen was setting in on a good cry by now. She knew what I had to do. She turned her back on me and lowered her head.

I aimed the gun at Runner's head. "I don't know what to say at a time like this, boy. 'Cept, you was always a good riding pony, and Pa is going to be heart broke when he hears what become of you." I sniffled and felt my resolve running out. "I'll miss you, old Runner." With that, I shot my Pa's pony in the head.

The shot done two things. It knocked me on my ass, and it rendered the darkness quiet. Could be my ears was ringing up a storm and blocking out any noise outside of my head, but it wasn't just the uproar of chatter and howling that was gone. It was the presence of things lurking in the shadows. They weren't just held out of sight by the shadows of the tunnel. They were gone.

"Let's go," I said scurrying to my feet. "Let's get our supplies and get out of here."

Doreen sprang into action and gathered up the bag of apples and her pack. She hesitated a moment to take in the sight of Runner's lifeless body, but she let the shock of it pass, and she tossed her belongings into the light. I grabbed the canteen of water and my pack and tossed them next to Doreen's.

"Pa's gonna want his saddle."

She looked at me like I was nuts.

"What? I can't just leave it." I reached down and worked the strap loose.

She shook her head in disbelief.

I sat down on the ground and propped my feet on Runner's back. Each foot was on either side of the saddle. I grabbed it by the horn and under the back of it, and I tugged and pulled and strained till the muscles in my shoulders felt like they were on fire. Out of breath, I said, "Help me."

Doreen moved around the other side of Runner and tried pushing on the saddle from her end while I pulled. It come forward a hair, but we couldn't manage no more than that.

"For a horse starved half to death, he sure is a fat cuss."

We heard a rock scoot across the riverbed deep in the darkest part of the tunnel. Doreen jumped. She backed away and pointed to the light.

"I can't. I lost Pa's pony. I ain't gonna lose his saddle."

A growl came out of the dark.

I jumped back this time and fought against my own awkwardness to get to my feet. "I 'spect he won't be needing a saddle if'n he ain't got a horse anyway."

Me and Doreen bolted for the light and stood next to our supplies as we stared into the tunnel.

"Worst part of losing Pa's pony is that them things in there is gonna eat him. Pa wouldn't want that. Hell, I don't hardly want that myself. Ain't dignified for a horse like Runner."

Doreen grabbed my arm and pointed into the darkness. A half dozen pair of lantern eyes were looking back at us. We hurriedly scooped up our things and ran like we was on fire.

I can't say how far we ran. It must have been a good piece because my thighs were burning. We climbed a small hill that didn't have a lick of grass, and I fell at its peak. I was too tired to get up, so I just laid there.

"It'll be dark soon enough. We should find even ground and camp. I ain't never been out this way, so I got no idea what we should be on the watch for. Billy used to go on about mountain lions and bears out this way. He's been known to exaggerate."

Doreen wasn't paying any attention to me. Something down at the bottom of the hill had her fixated. I scanned the land below and saw what had her in a trance, a tree.

"Lordy, would you look at that. A tree. I mean a real tree, big. That thing must be twenty feet high, easy." I stood still staring at the tree. "It's got leaves, too."

She giggled with excitement.

"Imagine that. Pa would do a dance for joy. That soils got yield, Doreen. It's got actual yield to it."

We barreled down the hill dragging most of our supplies behind us. There weren't no containing our happiness. We'd seen pictures of trees, big towering trees that reached up past the clouds, but the trees we had in Two Notch were nothing more than shrubs, and none of them had leaves. They had pine needles. I never thought in a thousand years that I'd actually see a tree that wasn't in a book or painting.

I touched the bark, half expecting it to hurt for some reason. It was rough and scaly. Doreen followed my lead. "Pa says trees is alive like you and me. He always said they had to be some still standing or else we'd all be dead. Trees is the reason we can breathe."

Doreen started to pet the tree like it was a horse or something.

"Old Kelly says God is the reason we can breathe." I laughed. "You can guess what Pa thinks about that."

She laid her cheek against the bark.

"Maybe they're both right. Somebody put this tree here. Why not God? God give us the tree. The tree gives us the air so we can breathe. Makes as much sense as anything else, don't it?"

She nodded again.

"I say we camp here."

She nodded.

I looked back up the hill. "Well, one thing about losing Runner. Means we both get three apples." I turned to her. "That there's what you call a silver lining. Pa says it's important to find the good in the bad and bad in the good. That way you can be thankful when it's called for, and on your guard when you really need to be."

There was some dead brush in the immediate area, so I built a substantial fire not too far from the tree. We wanted to be close to it, but we didn't want to choke it out with our smoke neither, so a spot back near the first slope of the hill seemed ideal. We sat and ate on our apples. We may should've rationed them out, but neither one of us knew how long apples kept. We figured the safest thing to do was to get them in our bellies before they went bad.

"Ever wonder where apples come from?"

Doreen was too busy eating to wonder about a thing like that.

"I ain't come across enough of 'em to ever ask. They're a fruit, right? So they come from the dirt in some way. I seen a strawberry growing right out of the ground once. Small thing. Pa grew it. Worked like the devil to get that thing to sprout up. He traded his whiskey rations for the extra water."

Doreen didn't appear to give two shits that Pa grew a strawberry.

"I reckon that's where the apples come from, too. Right out of the ground. That would be a sight, wouldn't it, a field of apples?"

She tilted her head and threw me a half smile.

I cocked my head back and took in the stars. "This time tomorrow we'll probably be met up with Abel Decker. It'll take us longer 'cause we're on foot now."

The air was crisp and taking on a chill. I could almost see my breath.

"I sure do feel bad about old Runner. Had him since I can remember. Ma got him from a traveling man that traded in meat. Roamed the country with a tiny herd of livestock. When he come to a town, he'd pick a horse or a goat or a skinny cow and trade it for gold piece by piece. When he'd run out of stock, he'd find a town running over with animals and trade gold for the livestock. You'd think he wasn't doing nothing but breaking even, but Pa says pieces of a horse is always worth more than the whole horse in this economy. Fact is the man wouldn't sell Pa the whole horse for a reasonable price. But Ma charmed him. She got Runner at market value. She had that way about her, according to Pa. I wouldn't know."

Doreen swallowed a bit of apple and belched.

I ignored her manners. "Yeah, I sure do feel bad about Runner." I took my eyes off the stars and yawned 'til my ears popped. "I have worked up an urgent need for sleep. I can promise you that." I leaned back and propped myself up on my elbows. I was so tired I didn't hear our approaching visitor. I become aware of her when Doreen stopped chewing her apple. She sat with the juices of the apple rolling out the corner of her mouth.

"What?" I said twirling around.

"Hello," said a stout blonde headed woman dressed in a ragged red sweater and tattered blue jeans.

I placed my hand on my Pa's army issue.

"Names Connie Benson." She saw where my hand had landed. "I'm friendly. Cold, but friendly."

I didn't move my hand.

"I got caught by the dark. Mistimed my departure."

I worked my way to my knees without letting leave of the gun.

"I saw your fire." She smiled. "I was hoping I could borrow a seat next to it."

"You alone?" I asked.

"I am."

"We ain't got no food to share."

She did a half turn to show me her backpack. "I do."

"Whatcha got?"

"Hardtack mostly, but I make mine with sugar."

I thought it over. I could tell by Doreen's face that she wanted some of that sugar bread. I finally nodded and give Connie Benson permission to sit.

She skipped around the fire and plopped down on the ground about an arm's length away from me. I found it in me to ease up a bit in my manner, and I sat with my arms wrapped around my knees.

"Where's your parents?"

"Doreen's a mute, barren girl whose ma died several weeks back. Don't know nothing about her Pa. My Ma's dead, too, but my Pa's alive. He's back in Two Notch trying to find the yield in the dirt. I'm Henry Arnaught."

"Two Notch?" She turned in the direction of our little city. "Are you telling me you're this far from your home without adult supervision?"

I thought about her question. "I don't know if I'm trying to tell you that or not, ma'am. I'm not 100% certain I know what adult supervision is."

She chuckled. "Young man, what I mean is, are you traveling alone?"

"We are."

She handed Doreen some of her sweet hardtack. "You came through Besser Pass?"

"Yes ma'am. That's the only way there is to get to Abel Decker's place from Two Notch."

"Abel Decker?"

"Yes ma'am."

"Now what would two adorable little children like you want with an immoral thug like Abel Decker?"

"Our town rector sent us. Old Kelly. She's says they're fucking marauders heading for Two Notch, and we're to hire Abel Decker for his services."

She rolled her eyes. "I cannot believe they have sent two children to make a deal with the devil himself."

"Pa was made to volunteer up our riding pony because ain't nobody else got one. Pa don't trust no one with the pony, so he sent me."

"And tell my why your father didn't just make the trek and leave you out of it."

"Broke his back in the war. He can't ride but a half mile or so before it pains him out of his mind."

She pursed her lips and shook her head. "Sounds like the war ruined his good senses, too. Sending you out here like this. And through Besser Pass to boot." She looked around. "Where is this horse of yours?"

"Lost him in the pass."

"Lost him?"

"He broke a leg, so I had to shoot him. I feel bad about that."

She gently placed her hand on my cheek. It was an appealing sensation. "Honey, you did what you had to do. That horse is better off."

"I know," I said. "But I still feel bad."

She pinched my cheek and stretched out her legs.

"What are you doing out here?" I noticed that her fingernails was painted up a blood red color.

"I was just on my way home after finishing up a job."

"Job?"

She waved her hand at me. "Just a thing I do for trade. Not important."

"My Pa says there ain't no jobs anymore."

She raised an eyebrow. "He's mostly right."

"He says 'bout the only people that's working is murderers, whores, and preachers."

She laughed. "Your Pa's back may be broken, but it appears he's still got his wits."

"Yes, ma'am."

"Well," she said tossing her hair back, "I've never killed anyone, and I threw my Bible out when I wasn't much older than you."

I considered her revelation. "Oh, you're a whore."

She laughed louder than she did before. "That's right."

I studied the flames popping out of the fire. "Pa never did explain what that was."

"Well," she said, "of the three professions that your daddy says is still in play, it's the only one that doesn't use fear to get the job done. I make people happy."

"That don't sound bad."

"Sweetie, it is so bad it's good."

I scratched my head. "That don't make no sense."

"I don't make the rules, kiddo. Your preachers and murderers do. I'm just a working girl trying to survive the tug and pull they got us all trapped in the middle of."

I shrugged because I had no idea what in the hell she was talking about. I got no opinion on the tugs and pulls of the world.

Doreen belched again, and that hit Miss Connie in the giggle reflexes.

"You're my kind of young lady, Doreen."

Doreen looked at her like she was seeing her for the first time. She blushed and turned away.

"She does that a lot."

"That's her prerogative."

"Yes, ma'am." I scrambled to find a new topic to discuss because I wasn't keen on talking about Doreen's belching habits. "You know Abel Decker?"

Miss Connie's forehead wrinkled, and she scrunched up her nose. "Goodness, no. But I know of his reputation. Knew a colleague who provided her services to him 'bout ten years back. Right when he came back from the war. A more frightful man you will not meet, she says."

"Frightful how?"

She pondered my question. "She didn't say exactly, but I got the sense the war had warped him. His mind wasn't right. They say he did terrible things over there. Killed nearly anything that walked or crawled or uttered a cross word."

I got the chills like she was telling us a ghost story. "I reckon the years have softened him somewhat."

"I'm afraid the years may have made him worse. The things he did probably dance around in his head like evil spirits, haunting him around the clock. He's likely gone mad trying to shut them down."

I was sorry I had traded this topic for Doreen's issues with gas. I hoped against hope she'd let out another burp so we could get back to it.

"They say he's got a brother. He's more or less Abel's handler. Keeps him in line, and helps him tend to his skills."

"Skills?"

"Killing."

"Oh, that."

"I assumed that is your town's interest in Mr. Abel Decker. They want him to kill the marauders."

"Fucking marauders," I said. "Old Kelly was clear on that point."

"Fine then, fucking marauders it is. The point is you've been sent to hire a killer to do what he does best."

"Yes, ma'am. I reckon you're right."

"Just out of curiosity what does a thing like that pay?"

"A barrel of water and three women."

"Not bad, but don't open with that."

"Ma'am?"

"Don't start off with your top dollar offer. Start off with the offer of a gal of his choosing first. He does get to choose, right?"

"Yes, ma'am."

"Good. Now he's likely to say no, but that's okay. The thing is with a fella like Abel Decker, he'll always start off with a no, regardless of what the offer is. It's just in his nature. It's in most men's nature. I could tell you a peck of negotiating horror stories. Every man I've ever come across seriously overestimates the value he brings to any deal. Understand?"

"Not really."

"Men think their shit don't stink. They got the idea that the world would cease to exist if they decided to not take part in it. It's by far the greatest flaw in nature. Now, thankfully, nature made men as stupid as they are arrogant. They can be worked like a farm mule with the right wiles."

Doreen smiled. She was enjoying the conversation.

"I ain't got no wiles, Miss Connie."

"Sure you do. You ain't a man yet. You're still a boy. A boy can outsmart a man any day of the week."

"They can?"

"I have no doubt. You see, a man is immediately put at a disadvantage because he assumes he is the smartest creature in any relationship. All you got to do is keep that in mind when you're negotiating with Abel Decker. Every word that comes out of his mouth is chosen so he can demonstrate his superiority. Let him have at it because a man will talk himself into bad deals without any assistance whatsoever."

I smiled. "Thanks."

She patted me on the head. "My pleasure. I just wish nature wasn't working against you. Everything I just told you will fade from your memory the second you become a man. You'll be just as stupid as the rest."

I gave her a cross look.

"Don't be mad at me, young Arnaught. Can't work against nature."

"Every once in a while nature shifts its ways. I seen a two-headed snake once."

She laughed. "I'll give you that, I suppose. I guess nature is a series of awful mistakes. Some are just less awful than others."

That made me think of poor old Runner. I felt real bad about shooting him.

8

I woke before the whore and Doreen. The sun hadn't peeked through yet, but the tiniest glow of it started to stretch up over the hill behind me. I wanted to see it rise up and take command of the day, so I climbed to the top of slope and set my eyes in the direction of the coming sunrise. I was not refreshed in the least. I had a fitful night's sleep. Every noise the dark makes seeped through my slumber and kept me on edge.

I turned toward Besser canyon where we he had emerged, where I shot Runner dead. I wasn't shocked to see that the horse was gone. I expect the lantern eyes drug him off to their den and ate him. Sons-a-bitches.

I felt the light from the rising sun on my face and turned to watch it float up, but stopped quick when I seen a flash come from the pass. It come again. I moved closer. Again. I narrowed my eyes, and waited for the flash to come again. There it was. It looked like... I rubbed my eyes. The sun was high enough to cast a good amount of light in that area. It was... It was my Pa's saddle. Sitting right there at the entrance to the pass.

I took a slow step toward it, examining every corner of the pass that I could see. It felt like a trap. Them lantern eyes was luring me back. I felt certain of it. They were gonna grab me soon as I stuck my hand in to pull the saddle out of the haunted dark of the pass.

My desire to retrieve the saddle trumped any concerns I had about the lantern eyes and their evil intentions. I took off in a good run and stopped five feet from the saddle. I was breathing heavy, more from the fright of it all than the power it took to run the distance I run. I set my eyes on every inch of the darkness, and didn't see lantern eyes one.

I worked to calm my nerves and then one, two, three jumped forward grabbed up the saddle and stumbled out into the growing light of the day. I fell flat on my face no more than six steps in my getaway. Busted my lip on the saddle horn. But, Lord as my witness, I didn't care a bit. I had my Pa's saddle. It would be something anyway. His disappointment would run deep on losing Runner, but I could tell him that I made sure to get his saddle. I went back for it. I didn't let my fear of the lantern eyes keep me from bringing it back to him. If'n he ever got a new horse, he wouldn't have to work a saddle into the trade. That's gotta count for something'.

As I got back to my feet, a growl from the pass put starch in my spine. I was too scared to run, and my knees wobbled and shook, and I may have peed myself the smallest bit.

I turned. There was two sets of lantern eyes looking back at me from the deepest part of darkness. Something come over me at that spot. Them eyes staring me down ate my horse. They put the fright in me that spurred me to drive Runner until he stepped wrong and broke his leg. They were the fuck all reason I was standing there holding my Pa's saddle and blood was coming out of my lip.

"You pleased with ya' selves?"

Their eyes seemed to grow small.

"That was my Pa's horse you ate! He was a fine horse. My Ma picked him out!"

The growling subsided.

I reckon this was where I cried a little. Not nothing I'm proud of. I ain't particularly ashamed of it neither. It is what is. I missed my Pa. I missed my Pa's horse. I missed my Ma who I never knew.

"How's my Pa gonna clear the land to find yield in the dirt without Runner? I can't do it. I ain't near strong enough." I was about to leave but stopped and yelled one more time, "That was my Pa's horse!"

The lantern eyes sank back into the dark and disappeared.

***

I wiped every speck of wetness from my cheeks before I stomped down the hill to our camp. Miss Connie had the fire going again, and Doreen was just sitting up and stretching the sleep out of her body.

Doreen perked up when she saw me and pointed to the saddle as I set it down.

"Appears lantern eyes ain't got no use for a saddle."

"Lantern eyes?" Miss Connie asked before seeing me. Then she said, "What happened to your lip?"

I touched it and said, "Fell."

"That can be hazardous."

"Ain't my normal practice."

"Good to hear. Now, what about these... what did you say? Ladder eyes?"

"No, ma'am. Lantern eyes, that's what we call the monsters in the pass."

"Fits." She reached into her backpack. "Since you two have been such wonderful hosts, I have a surprise for you." With that she pulled out three eggs.

Doreen went bug-eyed.

"They're hard boiled."

"Where in tarnation did you get a thing like that?"

"My last customer. He has six chickens."

"Six? We ain't got six chickens in all of Two Notch."

She handed an egg to Doreen and then me.

"I don't feel right eating your pay. I mean, you whored for this, didn't ya'."

She chuckled. "Son, the day I go boots up for three eggs is the day I will quit whoring. The customer was extra pleased with my work, so he gave me these eggs and a few other extras to show his appreciation."

I tapped the egg on a nearby rock. "You must be a good whore."

"Henry Arnaught, I am most likely the best whore left on this godforsaken planet."

"You seem to like it," I said peeling the egg.

"Love it, is more like it. It affords me luxuries in a world where necessities are rare."

I bit into my egg and was struck by the oddness of it. It felt like was I biting into a tasteless ball of soft rubber. I must of have showed my dissatisfaction in my face because Miss Connie commented on it.

"Don't like it?"

"Don't really taste nothing."

"That's cause you just bit into the white. The yolk should put a smile on your face. You've never had eggs before?"

"Not in this manner, ma'am. We don't have water enough for any kind of boiling."

She shook her head. "I declare. Two Notch is 'bout as backwoods as you can get, and this whole damn country is nothing but backwoods."

"You mean to say they're other towns that is better off?"

She bit into her egg and rolled her eyes. "Get to that yellow part and you'll be pleased."

"Yes, ma'am." I took a bigger bite and caught a bit of the yellow. It did have a taste to it, more so than the white.

"Not too many folks can afford my services in Two Notch, so I don't go soliciting there much, but the times I've been I can't say that it stacked up to every other town I've been to. No offense, I don't know why any marauders, fucking or otherwise, would want to bother with ransacking a dump like that."

I stuck the rest of the egg in my mouth. I wasn't too keen on it, but I needed the fuel, so I wanted to be done with it as quick as possible.

Doreen seemed to like hers.

"Old Kelly says they're coming for the children of Two Notch. Come to inscript them, or something."

Miss Connie considered what I had said and then belly laughed. "Child, I think you mean conscript. Means to call them up. Now, what would they be calling them up for?"

I shrugged. "The army I guess."

"The army? Federal?"

"Federal?"

She thought of the best way to clear up my confusion. "Is she referring to the armed forces that are in service to our country?"

"I ain't sure. I expect she means that. Our town gets piles of extra rations for every able body we send to the government to fight in the war. I imagine the marauders are coming for our able bodied to up their profits. "

Miss Connie shook her head. "Lord knows."

"What wrong, ma'am?"

"The army's been disbanded, Henry."

"Disbanded?"

"There isn't an army anymore."

"There ain't? How's that possible?"

"'Cause we ran out of enough able bodied folks, that's how. You can't build an army if you don't have healthy soldiers to kill. I'm not even sure there's still a government."

"We lost the war?"

"We did. They did. Nobody won. Technically, we're still at war. The battles are over, but the fighting isn't."

None of this information seemed to mean a thing to Doreen, but it had my head spinning. "That don't make a lick of sense, Miss Connie. There must be a war somewhere."

"When's the last time you lost some of your town folks to the government?"

I thought it over. "Don't know. Nine or ten years ago, I guess. I was too small to remember."

"That doesn't seem odd to you?"

"No, ma'am. I just figured they come through every nine or ten years."

"Your Pa didn't think it was odd."

"Pa don't talk much about nothing that's got to do with the war."

She took the last bite of her egg. "Just like a man. Burying his head in the sand."

"He ain't never done nothing like that, ma'am. He ain't afraid to stick his hands in the dirt, but he ain't never buried his own head."

She almost spit the egg out of her mouth. "Don't make me laugh with food in my mouth, Henry!"

"I didn't mean to."

She composed herself and swallowed. "Just how does this rector of yours know that fucking marauders are on their way to Two Notch?"

"God told her."

If she'd had egg in her mouth she would have spit it out for sure this time. "You're pulling my leg."

"No, ma'am, I ain't. That's the honest truth. Old Kelly gets messages set on her ears all the time by God. That's how come she's rector."

"This just gets better and better," Miss Connie said. "Henry Arnaught, I want you to do me a favor."

"Yes, ma'am."

"You gather up your things, and you take little Doreen there by the hand and go back to Two Notch."

"Ma'am?"

"You heard me. Go back to Two Notch. You don't have to go back through Besser's pass either. I'll show you a way around the canyon. It'll add a day or two to your trip, but it's better than running into those lantern eyes again."

"But I've got to hire Abel Decker for his services. Old Kelly give me the charge, and if'n I come back without him, they'll likely strip me and Pa of everything."

"Son, Old Kelly is a crazy old fool. God didn't tell her fucking marauders were on their way. You've been sent to face danger for no reason other than to satisfy a lunatic's delusions."

"Not sure what half of that meant, ma'am, but how do you know God didn't talk to Old Kelly?"

"Because, my sweet backwoods boy, God does not talk to anyone."

"He don't?"

"No."

"You know that for sure?"

She sighed. "I know very few things for sure. I know how to make a man's eyes roll back in his head with absolute pleasure. I know how to get a woman to dig her nails into a mattress and scream out in pure joy. I know that nobody even knows why we went to war in the first place, and I know without a shadow of a doubt that God does not talk to Old Kelly because God does not exist."

I raised an eyebrow. "My Pa says the same thing."

"That's the first sensible thing I've heard about your daddy."

I caught a glimpse of my Pa's saddle. If'n I went home, Runner died for nothing. I stood and brushed the dirt from my behind. "We best be going."

"Back to Two Notch, right?"

"No, ma'am. We got to see this thing through."

"Are you that stupid?"

"Yes, ma'am."

Doreen got on her feet and followed me to our pile of supplies.

"What about the girl? You're putting her life in danger."

Doreen didn't acknowledge the whore.

"I'm afraid she's twisted out of luck no matter what I do, Miss Connie."

"What do you mean?"

"She's barren. Her ma broke the law when she didn't put her down the second she found out. She ain't got but one purpose now, accompanying me on this trip. Old Kelly'd prefer if she expired along the way. But if by chance she survives, they'll find a way to dispose of her."

Miss Connie appeared to have the wind knocked out of her. "That's madness."

"I ain't happy about it, but there ain't much I can do. Females got to be able to contribute to our population first and foremost. If they can't they ain't got no use, and if they ain't go no use, they're just taking up rations unnecessarily. That's what Old Kelly says anyway."

I helped Doreen with her things and then packed up what I had to carry. Miss Connie was mumbling to herself and gathering up her own things.

"Henry Arnaught," she said, "I am mortified by very few things in this shit life on this shit planet, but what you have just told me has mortified me beyond belief."

"Sorry, ma'am."

"I don't blame you. Not one bit." She pointed at me as if she was scolding me, so it was hard to believe she didn't blame me. "I blame this Old Kelly and the spineless, feckless people of Two Notch."

"Yes, ma'am."

"That includes your daddy."

I wasn't as agreeable on that point.

"I'm coming with you."

"Ma'am?"

"You heard me. I'm coming with you to help you negotiate with Abel Decker, and then I'm escorting you to Two Notch. I'm going to have it out with this Old Kelly and reveal her as the fraud she is."

"That won't be easy."

"Why is that?"

"She's got men, ma'am. The biggest and meanest in town. They basically hold up her law. They've put down folks for looking at Old Kelly wrong. You're in for trouble if'n you got at Old Kelly with the kind of mad you got."

She slung her backpack over her shoulder and smiled. "Men? They're no match for my talents, Henry. Old Kelly may say she speaks to God to keep them in line, but five minutes with me, and they'll swear they're in heaven."

"Yes, ma'am."

She walked past us and started up the hill. "Hurry up. Time's a wasting."

Me and Doreen exchanged confused glances.

***

The trip was almost unbearable now that I had to carry my share of the supplies and Pa's saddle. It didn't appear to be that heavy when I first hoisted it up and started out, but it didn't take long for me to start cussing its very existence. The way to Abel Decker seemed to be met up with the occasional trips down the slope of hills. We walked and walked and walked for near two-hours before I couldn't go no more. We stopped at the bottom of yet another hill, and rested.

"Saddle's burdensome," I said having no luck catching my breath.

"Leave it," Ms. Connie said.

"Can't."

"Suit yourself, but this area doesn't see many travelers. It should be here when we get back."

"Can't chance it," I said. "Someone's likely to come along with my luck. It'd be different if there was someplace I could hide it, but this whole country ain't nothing but short brown grass."

"We got two more hills to climb and then we'll be at Tyler's Forest."

"That's nice."

"It's more than nice. It'll give you plenty of places to hide your daddy's saddle so you won't have to lug it any farther."

"How so?"

She looked totally bewildered by my question. "What do you mean? You'll hide it behind a tree or under a bush or whatever."

I was shocked. "You mean we're about to come upon another tree?"

She laughed. "Well, yes of course. What do you think a forest is?"

I looked at Doreen to see if that word meant anything to her and she shrugged. "I don't hardly know."

"Don't they have schools in Two Notch?"

"Yes, ma'am."

"And you don't know what a forest is?"

"We just talk about Old Kelly's law and parts of the Bible and such."

Miss Connie shook her head. "I really can't wait to meet that woman. A forest is a plot of land that is nothing but trees."

I didn't respond right away because I was waiting for her to start laughing. She was joking. There weren't no such thing as a plot of land with nothing but trees. That was about the craziest thing I'd ever heard.

Doreen stared at Miss Connie with wide eyes.

"Miss Connie," I said, "just 'cause we're a couple of kids don't mean we believe in nonsense like that."

"Nonsense?"

"There ain't no such thing as a bunch of trees on a plot of land. Maybe a long time ago, but not no more."

She shook her head. "What have they done to you children? I swear on my dead sister I'm telling you the truth."

I leaned back on my Pa's saddle. "It's a useless lie 'cause we're gonna know soon enough. Soon as we top that second hill and see nothing but brown grass and more hills, your lie will be easy enough to see."

"The only thing you're going to see is that you've been deprived of a proper education. The world isn't what your Old Kelly says it is."

***

We rested near a half hour before we took up our hike again. It give us time to chew on some hardtack and coyote jerky. I rationed out some water for me and Doreen and offered to share with Miss Connie, but she had her own. In fact, she had more water than I'd ever seen in one container. It was clear enough to see through, too. When I asked her where she got it, she said she didn't want to tell me.

"You'll just call me a liar again," she said.

I considered her concerns and said, "If it's a lie, I will, ma'am."

"There's a running stream that snakes through the forest," she said. "Water's clean and cold."

I shook my head. "I ain't gonna say it. I got a right to, but I won't."

"That's it,' She said standing. "On your feet, so I can show you that I'm not lying. And, young man, when you lay eyes on those big beautiful trees, the first thing that comes out of your mouth better be an apology."

"Yes, ma'am."

Off we went climbing the first of two hills. I brought up the rear toting Pa's saddle. My legs was aching from the extra weight and my grip was getting harder and harder to maintain. Before I felt bad for shooting Runner for Runner's sake, now I felt bad for shooting Runner for my sake. It didn't seem sensible on my part to expect a boy to carry what a horse normally does. But I was determined I wasn't gonna leave it out in the open where anyone could come up on it and snatch it.

At the top of the first hill, I paused while Doreen and Miss Connie made their way down. I could hear Miss Connie gabbing away, but I couldn't make out what she was saying. It didn't look like Doreen was paying her any mind at all.

I hoisted up the saddle and made my way down the hill. By the time I reached the bottom, Doreen and Miss Connie were at the top of second hill. The sun turned them into silhouettes. I couldn't make out what they were up to. I shielded my eyes with my hand and tried to catch a glimpse of their features, but the light was too blinding.

I repositioned the saddle and tried to get a better grip, but my hand cramped up on me. It felt like somebody was pushing a knife through my palm. I winced and dropped the saddle and massaged the bad hand with my good hand.

I heard a commotion coming my way, so I looked up. Doreen was barreling down the hill with a smile from ear to ear. She reached out, grabbed my cramped hand and tugged me up the mountain.

"Hold on, Doreen! My hand's all gnarled. I need a second or two to work it loose."

She kept on tugging.

"I can't leave the saddle!"

She stopped tugging and groaned in frustration. Then without no provocation from me she gave me a vicious pinch on the forearm. It caught me by surprise. Once I registered what she done, I planned on giving her a pinch of my own, but she was gone, lickitysplit, up the hill. And I chased after with every intention of pinching the shit out of her.

She reached the summit, and I was just a foot or two behind. "I'm gonna pinch you into next week, Doreen. I swear to all that is holy..." I stood on the summit, my arm still stinging a bit from Doreen's pinch and my hand still gnarled into a claw, staring down in amazement at trees, more trees than I could have ever imagined. Trees taller than most of the hills we had climbed to get here. It was just a blanket of trees as far as the eye could see spread out in every direction, sloping down into a huge valley.

"Told ya'," Miss Connie said.

"I can't see how this is hardly possible."

"What did I say?"

"Ma'am?"

"What are the words that should be coming out of your mouth, Henry Arnaught."

I grinned. "I'm sorry, Miss Connie. Glad to be sorry."

Doreen and Miss Connie helped me drag the saddle up the hill and down to the tree line. I hid it behind three fat towering trees and stacked branches and leaves on top of it until I was satisfied that it couldn't be seen even if you was standing next to it.

Miss Connie gathered me and Doreen at the entrance to the woods and said, "Abel Decker's place is only about three miles from here, but its three hard miles. We might want to wait 'til morning before we trek it."

"No, ma'am," I said. "They'll be expecting us back in a couple of days. Without Runner, that'll be tough enough to keep. If it's all the same to you, I'd like to keep going."

"I thought you'd say that." She took one last swig of her water and stepped onto the path.

I let Doreen go next and then I followed. Once we were far enough in that I could barely see the slope of the hill, I felt a touch of nerves. I looped my thumb under the strap of Pa's army issue just to remind myself it was there. I even mumbled his mantra a few times, "Red is for ammo. Blue is for pulse."

I soon learnt that forests move. The wind pushes shadows to and fro. The leaves on the trees twist and flutter about. And they're about a million different sounds competing for your audience. I wanted to ask Miss Connie if all this was normal, but I didn't want her to think I was scared or stupid.

The chill picked up the deeper we ventured into the woods. I broke out Pa's fox poncho, and helped Doreen on with hers.

We walked without saying a word for as long as I could stand it. I got tired of hearing the woods taunt me, so I begun to hum up a storm. I didn't know no particular song, so I just hummed the melody that come to me. Miss Connie didn't have no use for it.

"Must you, Henry?"

"No, ma'am," I said. "Just bored that's all."

"You know what I like to do when I'm bored?"

"How would I know a thing like that?"

She ignored my biting tone. "I like to think, quietly."

"No offense, but that seems twice as boring."

I noticed the labor in her breathing as she talked. "Thinking, young man, is the least from boring that you can get. The mind can entertain you for countless hours if you work it right."

"I 'spect that's my problem then. I don't know how to work my mind."

"That is a distinct possibility. I'll give you a start." She mulled over a topic in her mind and then said, "I like to think about before the war."

"Before the war?" I peeked around Doreen at Miss Connie's behind as she stepped over a bundle of roots. She held onto her figure pretty good for someone who can remember all the way back before the war. "I ain't pegged you for that old."

She laughed. "I'm not that old, silly, but I did grow up with my grandmother. She was fifteen when the war started."

"Was she a whore, too?"

Miss Connie stopped walking, which caused Doreen to trip and near fall, which caused me to run smack into the back of her. I grabbed her poncho and kept her upright once I claimed my own balance. "Don't say things like that about my grandmother, you here?" She gazed at me like I just punched her granny in the mouth.

"Didn't mean no disrespect."

She studied my face. I half expected her to slap me.

"I didn't know it was a bad thing."

She eased the hate from her face. "It's not... exactly. It's hard to explain."

"Don't sound hard. Either it's bad or it ain't."

"Ahhh, young Henry, I see you dwell in the land of absolutes."

Doreen snickered more because of the way Miss Connie sounded all snooty when she said what she said than for what she said. I was pretty sure she didn't understand what dwelling in the land of the absolutes meant no better than I did. "No, ma'am. Least ways I don't think so."

She caught on to my confusion. "That means you see things as black and white."

This time I snickered. "I see colors."

"No," she said with a bit of flare in her voice, "you see things as either right or wrong. There are no in betweens for you."

"Oh," I said, "that kind of absolute. I guess if a thing ain't wrong it's right, and the other way around, too."

"You mean to say that you've never done something that was wrong for the right reasons."

"Don't know what you mean."

She grabbed hold of a small tree and pulled herself up a steep incline and then turned to help Doreen up. "If you're Pa was starving, would you steal food to feed him."

I climbed the rise. "Well, it'd be wrong to let my Pa starve."

"But stealing is wrong, too."

I gave her point considerable thought. "S'pose one things less wrong than the other."

She clasped her hands together and raised them above her head, "Lord, he has seen the light."

"So, whoring was more wrong in your granny's time?"

"It was judged more harshly by more people. Let's put it that way. The reasons someone would whore themselves out then are the same as today, the circumstances are just different."

"Meaning?"

"Meaning we're faced with a whole different level of desperate than they were. Goes back to what your daddy said about the state of employment these days. Those other two occupations he mentioned... I've got no interest in selling my soul to qualify for one, nor do I wish to kill someone to qualify for the other. That leaves me with one desperate choice. And that is just a matter of me renting my body out for an hour here and there."

"So people weren't desperate before the war?"

"No, they were. They just didn't have near the reason we do. Whores weren't the best of three choices. They fell down the pack a good ways in the face of millions of opportunities. People could literally get paid to do just about anything."

I laughed. I'd never heard anything so ridiculous.

"Just what's is so funny?"

"No offense, Miss Connie, but that don't sound possible to me."

"No one has ever told you about the world before the war?"

"No one in their right mind."

"You're Pa never bothered to pass along this kind of information?"

"He said something about people playing something called football, but that's about it."

She moaned. "Just like a man. Talk about the one profession that didn't do the world any good. People used to get paid to care for other people, teach other people, make them beautiful, make them laugh, fix their teeth, you name it, people got paid for it."

I ran my fingers across my front teeth. I tried to think of something totally useless to test her claims. I pulled my hand away from my mouth and noticed the dirt caked under my fingernails. "What if'n I wanted my fingernails tended to and cleaned?"

"People paid for that, and to get them painted, too."

I rolled my eyes. "My Pa's got a wart on his butt. You saying he could trade to have that removed?"

Doreen covered her mouth and giggled.

"First of all, yuck. And second of all, he wouldn't trade to have it done. He would pay someone to have the wart removed, a skin doctor."

"Skin doctor?" I waved her off. Why in the hell would someone doctor skin? "No, offense, Miss Connie, but I expect your granny was telling you fairytales about the way things used to be."

She stopped and half ducked.

"Miss Connie…"

"Shhhh," she said getting down even lower.

A gust of wind caught me in the face. I stooped over and yanked Doreen down.

Miss Connie turned and directed us to quietly move up next to her.

Kneeling down beside her, I zeroed in on what had her so spooked. A massive brown mat of fur rumbled through the forest about thirty feet or so ahead of us.

"Bear," Miss Connie whispered.

I held back a giddy grunt. I had heard all about bears, but I ain't never seen more than a tooth or two from one in my lifetime. I'd been told you would have to walk for weeks before you'd ever come upon one.

Miss Connie stuck her finger up in the air. "Wind's blowing towards us. We'll be fine if we stay still."

I was amazed at how big it was. It was pert near the size of poor old dead Runner. It sauntered about and sniffed the ground, stopping occasionally to dig through some rotten wood. Every once in a while I caught a glimpse of its big hooked claws. They were as imposing, if not more than the teeth I had seen. It looked our way once or twice, but didn't spy us through the brush. It lifted its nose up in the air and sniffed, but the wind carried our scent in the other direction.

Fifteen minutes passed after the bear moved out of sight before Miss Connie stood up. "It's safe."

"You sure?" I asked.

"Pretty sure." She stepped forward and snapped a stick in half on the trail.

The sound of it was the tiniest of sounds. It wasn't even loud enough for us to take notice. But what's small to us must be a blaring trumpet to a bear 'cause a violent roar raised up out of the trees.

Miss Connie stepped back and held her arms out wide to keep us from moving past her. She was still as a stone.

The roar carried on a bit. It seemed like it was bouncing from tree to tree. We didn't see no movement.

It was enough to make us think the bear wasn't calling out in response to that itty-bitty stick breaking.

But our hopes was dashed when the bear's snout pushed through a bush. It was sniffing like it was crazy hungry.

Its massive head tilted up and its deep brown eyes laid dead on us.

We all gasped together.

"What do we do?" I asked.

Miss Connie didn't say nothing. She just grabbed hold of our arms and stepped back.

The bear raised up on two legs and pointed its nose directly at us.

"Miss Connie…"

She was white as can be. "Children," she said still dragging us back. "Run!"

And run we did. In all different directions. We lost our minds with fright. I zipped off to the right stumbling over roots and rocks and anything else the forest laid out in my path. I looked over my shoulder once to see what had become of Doreen and Miss Connie, but they weren't nowhere to be seen. I thought I heard a scream, but it could have been any number of things. Hell, it could have even been me screaming.

I ran and stumbled and fell to the ground on more than one occasion. It wasn't till the third time I was picking myself up that I realized I still had Pa's army issue. It didn't make me feel no better about my situation. The way the gun kicked me around when I shot Runner in the head had me doubting my ability to take down a charging, man-eating bear. In fact, I considered tossing it aside. It wasn't doing nothing but slowing me down. I looped the strap over my head and studied it.

"Nice gun," a man's voice said.

I looked up the path in front of me and a short, fat squat figure of a man with a bushy brown beard was staring at me with a creepy grin.

"Where'd you get it?"

I didn't answer.

"That there's army issue, son."

I nodded.

"Now if the Army's digging down deep enough in the population to draft the likes of you, then I reckon they should disband."

I didn't reply.

"Ain't 'cha got nothing to say?"

"Bear," is all I could manage to spit out.

He squinted one eye. "Possum."

I cocked my head to the right. "Sir?"

"Ain't we naming off animals?"

I shook my head. "No sir there's a bear chasing me and a whore and a mute girl named Doreen."

He smiled. "Well, that there sounds like a party, but I'll be straight up with ya', boy, I don't see a whore or a mute girl named Dorris."

"Doreen."

"Very well, Doreen. The point is you're alone. The companions you speak of are not in your company. That poses some credibility problems for you, son."

"They were. The bear scattered us."

"What bear?"

"It must have gone after Doreen or Miss Connie."

He stroked his beard. "I suppose I can concede that this bear ran after one of your female cohorts. That makes your story slightly more believable. I still have a small problem with this tale of yours."

"What's that?"

"I think it's more like the bear was chasing you."

"Me?"

He motioned for me to turn around. When I did, I was shocked half to death to see the black flaring nostrils of the bear just inches from my face. For some fool reason, I laughed. The bear was so startled by my reaction it jerked back. I felt a wave of numbness travel up my body. My legs wobbled. The more I fought to stay on my feet, the darker the world got. I was out cold before my knees buckled and I fell flat on my back.

***

I come to with my head spinning like a top. The bearded man was leaning over me saying something, but I couldn't tell you what. I could tell you that he stunk like skunk shit. It was apparent to me that I hadn't been eaten by the bear, but taking in the stranger's odor, I wished I had.

A steady ringing in my ears started to fade and I could make out what the man was saying, "Wake up, son. C'mon now."

I blinked and breathed for what felt like the first time in my life. A heavy pressure lifted from my lungs.

"That's it. Breathe."

I tried to say, "Bear," but it must have come out all jumbled because the man appeared puzzled.

"Henry," I heard Miss Connie say.

The fat bearded man looked up. "Over here."

The brush rustled and popped and Miss Connie come stomping up on us.

"Get away from him," she said.

"He fainted dead away."

I wanted to tell her I didn't. That it was a damned lie. I didn't faint. I passed out. Sissies faint. But, I couldn't work up the breath to convey my concerns at his mischaracterization.

"I said get away from him," she said.

The stranger chuckled and stood up. She was kneeling by my side quick as a wink.

"Doreen," I managed to say.

"She's here," Miss Connie said motioning for the mute girl to join her.

She practically hopped next to me. Before I knew what was happening, she bent down and laid a kiss on my forehead.

I grimaced and sat up. "Whatcha do that for?" I asked wiping away Doreen's slobber. A warm rush of disgust washed away the dizziness.

"You must be the whore," the stranger said.

Miss Connie laid the evil eye on him.

"Don't take offense. That's what the boy called you. I meant it as a term of occupation not as a statement on your character."

Her gaze eased a tad. "I do whore for a living, but don't get any ideas. I'm not on duty."

"Taking a vacation, are ya'?"

"I'm looking after these children who've been sent on a fool's mission by a fool rector and a town full of dangerously dull citizens."

"That's quite the task."

"And who might you be a fat busybody?"

He raised an eyebrow and stroked his thick beard. "I might be that, yes. Or I might be a thief or a murdering bandit or a cannibal. I might be a lot of things. World's full of might-bes capable of unthinkable acts."

Miss Connie clutched me and Doreen by the shoulders.

The stranger smiled. "But you can rest easy, because I'm just a hunter out on the prowl with my friend Bob trying to scare up fresh meat."

Miss Connie eased her grip. "And where is this friend of yours?"

He hesitated and then said, "Now, I could tell you that, but I'm kind of afraid to."

"Afraid?"

"Yeah, you see the boy here got one look at Bob, and he fainted before I could explain Bob's true nature."

I swallowed. "Bob is the bear?"

"On the surface," the Stranger said. "But Bob ain't really bear-like in his demeanor."

"Wait a minute," Miss Connie said. "Are you saying that bear is your pet?"

"Oh no, ma'am. Bob's a friend."

"A friend?" Miss Connie squeezed our arms again. I had a feeling she was considering the fact that the fat bearded stranger was a complete loon. I had that feeling because I was thinking the same thing.

The stranger smiled. "Won him in a poker game 'bout five years back. Some circus fella' banked on a straight before the draw when I was holding two pair. He didn't get his eight. I got the bear. Named him Bob 'cause I liked the sound of it, Bob the bear."

"He's trained then?" Miss Connie asked.

"He is, but mostly for useless stuff. Walking on two legs, dancing, standing on his head. Humiliating shit for a bear."

"He don't eat people?" I asked.

"No, he does." The stranger reared back and let out a whistle. "Well, I should say he's eaten a person. The circus fella who I won him from to be exact. First thing he done when I let him loose from his chains. Barreled right for the poor bastard."

"And you just let him?" Miss Connie asked.

"Hell, yes, I let him. First off, he was starved near half dead by that jack-ass who kept him. Second off, I was grateful he wasn't eating me. And third off, and this is probably most important of all, that circus fella had been cheating that whole card game. I just outwitted him on that last hand. He got what was coming to him."

Bob the bear entered the path behind the stranger and lumbered torward us. Me, Miss Connie, and Doreen tensed up.

"He ain't gonna hurt ya'," the stranger said.

Miss Connie said in an unsteady voice, "How can you be so sure?"

"'Cause he's full for one thing. I keep him fat, so he won't feel tempted to break our bond. And he ain't near as angry as he used to be. I set him loose in these woods as soon as I got back from the poker game and he's had the time of his life doing as he pleases. Something about freedom and food that makes a bear as docile as a kitten."

Doreen pulled herself away from Miss Connie and approached the bear despite our best efforts to call her back. She reached out and tugged on the bear's fur under its chin. The giant animal snorted and licked her face.

"You see," the stranger said. "Docile as a kitten."

Miss Connie breathed easier.

I stood and tentatively approached the bear.

"Now, just what is the fool's mission you kids have been sent on?" The stranger asked.

"Our town's in trouble," I said reaching up and scratching behind the bear's ear. "Our rector sent us to bring back help."

"What kind of trouble?"

"Fucking marauders," I said barely paying attention to what I was saying. The bear was mesmerizing.

"So, it's hired guns you'll be needing."

"One hired gun," I said.

"One?"

"A man named Decker."

There was a moment of silence before the stranger said, "I'm a man named Decker."

10

"Ike Decker's the name." The fat man sat his plump ass down and leaned against a tree. "And I 'spect I ain't the Decker you're looking for."

"You 'spect right," I said.

"You're Abel Decker's brother?" Miss Connie asked.

"That I am. We share a spread 'bout a mile and half from here."

Bob the bear was lying on his back while Doreen rubbed his belly. He huffed and groaned and gave every indication that he was enjoying the hell out of that belly rub.

"What's this rector of yours willing to trade for Abel's services?"

I hesitated and looked at Miss Connie. She had said to start off low in the negotiating with Abel Decker, but this was his brother. I wasn't exactly sure where to start with him.

"I think it's best we present the terms to Abel," Miss Connie said with a smile.

Ike pulled a cigarette from his shirt pocket. "I handle my brother's affairs. You present the terms to me, and I'll present them to him. Works like that." He stuck the cigarette in his mouth and lit it with a fancy lighter taking a deep draw.

Miss Connie gave me a nod.

I prepared to make my first offer when I caught a whiff of the smoke coming off the cigarette. It was different than any cigarette I had ever smelled before. It was sweeter and made its way to the back of my throat. "Cigarette's gone bad," I said coughing.

He smiled. "Ain't nothing wrong with the cigarette, boy. This here's an adult cigarette."

"Adult?" I pondered his description. "I ain't never seen a kid smoke no kind of cigarette, not my age anyway."

"Well, you definitely won't see them smoke this kind, not unless they're trouble. You remember that. Never let your lips touch this kind of cigarette until you're fifteen or sixteen."

Miss Connie cleared her throat and rolled her eyes.

"Don't want to corrupt the young, miss whore... lady. Just trying to set him on the right path." He took another drag and held the smoke in his lungs. After releasing it he said, "The terms, boy. The terms."

I swatted the smoke away from my face. "The town's prepared to give you a barrel of water."

Ike nearly choked on a throat full of smoke. "Water? What the hell? Water ain't in short supply around here."

"It ain't?"

"Not at all. Got two babbling brooks that crisscross my property."

"Oh."

"Hope you got something else."

"You got ladies on your property?"

The funny smelling cigarette dangled from his mouth and he squinted against a stream of smoke rising off the end. "Now, I must admit we are in short supply of that particular resource."

I smiled.

"I can offer you a lady."

"A lady?" He took the cigarette from his mouth. "Just like that. You're going to give me a person."

"No, sir, your brother."

"All the same. You're rector is giving out ladies?"

I shrugged. "I reckon."

He laughed. "Now if that ain't the bottom of the moral bucket, I don't know what is. A rector, a person of godly pursuits, has sent a boy and girl no bigger than sand bags on a dangerous trip to sell a lady to a man who kills people for a living." His laughter grew more and more intense. "If that ain't the ever-loving shit of all shits."

I didn't get the joke. "I can make it two ladies."

This new information caused Ike to laugh even harder.

Miss Connie patted me on the shoulder.

He struggled to right himself from all that laughing. "These ladies… they good stock?"

"Don't know what you mean. I ain't got no idea how to stack a lady up that way. Anyway, the rector says Abel Decker can have his pick."

"Abel ain't got no interest in that sort of thing. Course, I wouldn't mind a little female companionship. Been over to Evendale three times trying to find me a pretty or not so pretty lady to come home with me. Struck out every time. In all my trying, it didn't never occur to me to buy a lady. I mean for more than hour… no offense," he said to Miss Connie.

"None taken. And it's a shame it didn't occur to you to buy yourself a companion in Evendale. I know of three dealers off the top of my head."

"Really?" He looked dumbfounded.

"Male, female, fat, skinny, you can get just about anything."

He sucked on his cigarette. "Lord, what has the world come to. There was a time that was frowned upon. Person could go to jail for that sort of thing." He looked at his cigarette. "Course a person could go to jail for smoking one of these, too." His eyes focused on the glowing red, burnt end of his cigarette. "I guess living in a lawless society has its pluses and minuses."

"Does that mean you accept my offer?"

"I am tempted," he said standing. His knees buckled a bit and he swayed slightly. "It has come to that. I'd have to interview the ladies at length. Don't want someone I ain't compatible with. Got to have a connection. Just 'cause I'm buying her don't mean I ain't a romantic."

Miss Connie said, "I don't mean to be a stickler for details, but the boy is hiring your brother. He's the one who will receive the trade, not you."

"Told you," he said. "It's all the same. Abel acts on my counsel. You've made an attractive offer. It crosses a moral line that I have never before considered, but I realize now that I have not considered it because I have never been presented with it. Apparently my objection to such a practice was merely an abstract objection. Push has come to shove, and I find myself helplessly salivating over you proposal."

I scratched the back of my head. "Does that mean your brother is hired for Two Notch?"

Ike stuck out his fat hand for me to shake. "It does indeed."

11

We arrived at Ike and Abel's spread shortly after night fall. Bob the bear trailed us the whole way. It sets your teeth on edge a bit to have a massive man-eating bear dogging you in the woods as the sun sinks out of the sky, especially when the bear has a tendency to grunt and growl from time to time. Ike said it was his way of breaking the silence. I didn't much care for his way.

The spread was just that, a spread of land beset by forest on every side. Ike said it stretched out about ten square acres. It was as green as the trees that outlined it. The grass was tall and bent at the wind's whims. And, just as Ike had claimed, the land was crisscrossed by two babbling brooks. They were about six foot at their widest. It was all I could do to not just plop myself down in the middle of the running water and let it wash all over me.

I heard a horse whinny and looked to my right. Bob the bear was walking up on four horses. These horses weren't nothing like Runner. They were big and well-fed. I expected Bob to rear up and pounce on one at any second. Instead, he just ambled past them and sat down on a worn piece of ground.

There was a big house at the back of the property with a smaller cottage next to it. Ike said he and Abel had built the two structures themselves. The bigger house was Ike's and the cottage belonged to Abel.

"He don't venture out of it too much anymore," Ike said. "Likes to keep to himself."

"How does he take to visitors?' I asked.

"Ain't had one in near three years, so I can't say for sure."

"How'd he take to it then?"

"Not altogether terrible. It was a fella who earned food in trade for chores and such. I wasn't around when he showed up. Abel greeted him. Didn't want to hire him, though. Apparently, the man took to begging. Abel don't have much of a tolerance for begging."

I come close to asking Ike to not carry on with his story, but the wrong part of me was curious to know what Abel did in response to something he ain't got tolerance for.

"I got home and found the fella curled up in a ball on the edge of the property with both his ears cut off. When I asked Abel why he done such a thing, he said the man's ears weren't doing him no good because he couldn't hear Abel tell him no over and over again. I patched the fella' up and fed him supper before I sent him on his way. I figured two ears was good for a meal. Fair exchange."

"Fair exchange?" Miss Connie said with a look of fright.

"You call that not altogether terrible?" I asked.

Ike shrugged. "If the fella had come through here right after my brother got back from the war, Abel would have gutted him 'fore he asked for work. Time has mellowed him."

A light flickered on in the cottage, and I saw the huge shadow of a man walk past the window.

Ike studied the little structure and then turned to us with a nervous glare in his eyes. "Y'all best keep back. Maybe over by the horses. I gotta prepare Abel for your visit." He lifted a hand to scratch his beard. He was shaking.

Miss Connie said, "You that scared of your brother?"

He let out a nervous chuckle. "I ain't talked to him in three months. As far as I know, he ain't stepped outside in all that time. To be honest with you, I don't know how he's been eating. The cold storage with all our food is underneath my house."

"Three months?" Miss Connie glanced at the cabin and then at us. "We should do as Ike says, children."

Me and Doreen grabbed onto her hands and walked with her over to the horses. Ike waited until we came to a stop before he turned and made his way to the cottage. He was moving slow with his head hung low. I didn't have much hope of us leaving the area alive if Abel's own brother was this scared of him.

At the door to the cottage, Ike lifted his hand and knocked. Nothing happened. He knocked harder and yelled out, "Abel, it's Ike."

The shadow passed the window on the way to the door. My heart jumped as I heard the door squeak open. There stood a giant of a man. He looked to be two heads taller than Ike. He wasn't fat like this brother, but he was broad and thick. It was hard to believe Ike and Abel were the same species let alone brothers.

Ike spoke. He was too far away to make out words, but I could tell by his manner that he was making a mess of our request. He was falling all over himself to not say the wrong thing and set Abel off. He got done speaking and the darkening night filled with the low rumble of Abel's voice. He only got out a sentence or two before he slammed the door in Ike's face.

Ike stood on the stoop like a lummox for a beat or two and then bounded toward us. To our surprise, he had a smile on his face. "You're in luck. He said he'd think it over."

"Really?" I asked with a hint of merriment in my voice.

"Kind of," Ike said. "He didn't say he wouldn't anyway."

"What did he say?" Miss Connie asked.

Ike mulled over her question and then said, "He more or less said he'd kill me if I knocked on his door again."

"And you're happy about that?" she asked.

"Hell, I usually can't get him to answer the door. Means he must've seen you from the window and was curious."

I spent the rest of the night trying to feel good about the fact that Abel Decker was curious about me.

***

Ike fed us pretty good. He had a mess of venison in his cold storage and he rustled up some fried potatoes and baked up some honest to goodness bread. It was soft and spongy and was just about the furthest thing from hardtack I had ever tasted. He even had butter, sweet smooth butter.

"Got a couple of goats that come and go off the property. I don't necessarily own them, but they come by because I put out feed."

"And Bob don't bother them?" I asked.

"Bob won't take animals on my property. Can't tell you why exactly. I ain't never directed him not to, not that I could if I tried. Somehow he knows. Now, if Bob was to see one of them goats in the woods, he'd take'em down and gobble' em up quick as shit."

I shoved a piece of venison in my mouth and sank my teeth into the tender meat. It nearly knocked me out it tasted so good. "This is the finest meal I have ever had," I said.

Doreen flashed a big smile across her face.

"Reckon this is one of them happy meals I was telling you about, Doreen."

She giggled.

"She your sister?" Ike asked.

"Nope. Ain't got a sister or brother or nothing but my Pa."

"Girlfriend?"

"Lord, no," I said. "She's ain't nothing to me 'cept a traveling companion. Old Kelly sent her with me to keep me company on my trip."

"She sent a mute girl with you to keep you company on your trip?"

"Yep."

"And this Old Kelly is your rector?"

"She is."

Ike poured some whiskey into a tin cup. "How is it she knows that marauders are descending on Two Notch?"

"Fucking marauders."

"Padon me?"

Miss Connie grinned. "He does that."

"Just following Old Kelly's words. She said I was to say exactly what she said. She was clear on the fucking marauders title."

Ike tipped his cup at me. "Okay, then how is it that Old Kelly knows that fucking marauders are descending on Two Notch?"

"God told her."

Ike stopped mid-sip of his whiskey and eyeballed me. "Come again?"

"God set a vision upon her," I said. "He does that with her from time to time."

"You was sent through hell and high water to find my brother because of a vision?"

"Hard to believe, isn't it?" Miss Connie said. "That's Two Notch for you. Backwards. Backer than backwards."

Ike sipped his whiskey. "Well, let's not tell Abel that. Visions by the ministry don't set too well with him. I seen him beat a preacher silly for suggesting that Jesus would save the world."

"I take it he's not a religious man," Miss Connie said.

"It ain't so much that. He just ain't too fond of the clergy always trying to drag God and Jesus and Allah and whatever else you got into our shit. I don't think he believes they should be sullied in such a manner."

Miss Connie smiled. "Amen to that."

Ike yawned. "Well, spiritual matters aside, I am plum tuckered. You're welcome to bed down wherever you like. I got me a spring mattress in the back room." He stood, took one last sip of whiskey and slammed the cup on the table upside down.

"The children and I will clean up the dishes," Miss Connie said.

"Well, now. That would be much appreciated. Maybe after you can come down and try out my mattress. Got lots of bounce." He winked at her and then said, "No children. Spring mattresses ain't for the young."

"I'll be fine out here," Miss Connie said.

He frowned and staggered to the back room.

Doreen grabbed his plate and started piling food on it.

"Whatcha doing?" I asked.

She didn't answer of course. She just continued to pile scraps of meat and potatoes and bread on the plate until it was about two inches high. She carried the plate across the room and went out the side door of the house.

Miss Connie and me followed.

Doreen stepped off the step, walked about ten feet toward the back corner of the house and set the plate down. Bob the bear appeared around the corner and immediately started lapping up the food.

"Looks like Doreen's made a friend," Miss Connie said.

"I reckon he's a good one to have."

Miss Connie watched the bear eat for a few minutes and then ducked back inside the house to clean up as she had promised Ike. I was about to join her when I saw a coin sized amber glow coming from the front porch of the cottage. It moved up and down a few times before I figured out what it was. Abel Decker was smoking a pipe. The darkness covered his features, but I could tell from the direction he was sitting that he was watching Doreen feed Bob. Even the shadow of him shook me up.

I watched him for probably five minutes. I counted the number of times he brought the pipe up to his mouth, twenty-two. He never changed his motion. It was the same over and over again, like he was one of them robots I had heard some of the folks in town talk about. According to them, robots ain't got no feelings or variety in the way they do things. They get taught a task and do the task just as they were taught. It looked like Abel Decker didn't know but one way to smoke a pipe. That one way scared the piss out of me.

***

I slept on the floor on the opposite end of the front room from Miss Connie and Doreen. They were talking to each other. I guess Miss Connie felt motherly around Doreen. She took it on herself to pay special mind to her. I ain't sure what Doreen felt for Miss Connie. She seemed to like having her around. Probably because she was an adult that didn't treat her like a wasted body. But, I ain't sure if she felt anything at all. She was more than mute. Her mind appeared quiet, too.

I fell asleep with Pa's army issue by my side and the image of Abel Decker smoking that damn pipe of his. I played the sight of it in my mind. The glowing amber going up and down, up and down, up and down, until it played heavy on my brain. That heaviness turned to sleep. When I first heard his footsteps, I thought it was a dream. His boots thumped the wood floors of Ike's house as he entered the front door and walked across the entrance to our pile of belongings.

I opened my eyes a slit and saw the giant man stooped over our things. He picked up an article of clothing and tossed it aside. He picked up a canteen, opened it, and sniffed the contents. He picked up Doreen's canvas bag that held the apples. I could tell by the way his knuckles turned white that he was gripping it tight. He reached in and pulled out an apple core. He let out a soft groan. He wasn't too happy.

He turned his face to me, and I got my first good look at Abel Decker. He was hard in expression. Tiny wrinkles jetted out from the corners of his eyes. Gray stubble dotted his face. His jaw was clenched and muscular. His eyes were dark, made darker by a thick brow. If I could make a face that would scare the devil back to hell, it would be Abel Decker's face. It ain't that he was ugly. His face was just set in hate.

He turned and walked to the door. Before exiting, he said, "Dumbass kids. You ain't supposed to take the apples." He walked out the door.

I breathed. I must have been breathing while he was in the room, but the second he left it felt like I took my first breath in hours. I stood up and walked over to Miss Connie and Doreen. They were still asleep. I worked my way as close to them as I could get without touching them, and laid back down.

I didn't have no idea what he meant about the apples. Didn't put much thought into it. All I could think about was that hateful face of his. I was beginning to think Old Kelly wasn't right in the mind. Only a crazy person would call up Abel Decker for help.

***

I woke up to the sound of bacon sizzling in the kitchen. Miss Connie and Ike were laughing up a storm. I pushed myself up off the floor and stumbled towards the sound with my eyes half closed. The smell of the bacon smacked me in the face as soon as I entered the room, and I smiled without thinking. Ike stood over the pan and tended to the cooking. Miss Connie and Doreen were sitting at the table.

"There he is," Miss Connie said. Doreen was sitting next to her piling jam on a fluffy, flaky biscuit.

"Sit down, little man," Ike said. "Got bacon, eggs, biscuits, and potatoes with wild onions."

I plopped down on a chair. "You sure do eat good out here."

"Hell, boy, you think I got this figure starving to death."

"Reckon not." I yawned.

Miss Connie reached over and wiped the sleep from my eyes. "I noticed you found your way across the room last night."

I didn't want to tell her I was scared, so I come up with the best lie I could. "Got cold when Abel opened the door last night."

Ike lost interest in the bacon. "Abel opened the door?"

I nodded. "Come in and went through our stuff."

Miss Connie looked horrified. "Did he take anything."

"No. He was just curious was all. I reckon he was just trying to find out more about us."

She huffed. "Normal people do that by engaging in conversation."

I didn't bother reminding her there wasn't nothing normal about Abel.

"He say anything?" Ike asked.

"Well, he got a might irritated when he found our apple bag."

"Apple bag?" Ike asked.

"Doreen found it in Besser Pass."

Ike looked a bit irritated himself. "Besser Pass? Oh, Lord. You took the apples?"

"What?" I asked.

"That was a shit dumb thing to do, is what." Ike turned back to the bacon. "Shit dumb."

I looked at Doreen. She didn't seem to be paying attention to the conversation. "There wasn't nobody around laying claim to 'em."

"I can't believe those piss-fool people of Two Notch sent you through Besser Pass without telling you about the apples."

"Not everybody knows about the apples," Miss Connie said. "Most who do say it's a myth."

"Well that's shit dumb, too," Ike said.

"What so danged important about the apples?" I asked.

Ike removed the skillet from the stove and walked over to the table, holding it while the bacon continued to pop and sizzle. "They're special apples, boy. The Ancients leave them about in the pass for day travelers."

"The Ancients?"

"The people of the pass. They went underground the first days of the war. Religious folks. Not like your rector. They ain't in it for the spoils. They're in it for the sacrifice of the flesh for the riches of the soul. You understand?" He set the skillet down in the middle of the table and sat in the chair across from me. His beard was coated in bacon grease.

"Not exactly."

"Material belongings mean less than nothing to these people. They hold onto the notion that someone who clings to things is evil, Satan himself. Now, I don't know what you know about Satan, but he ain't liked by religious folks. Not in the least."

"What's Satan got to do with me and Doreen?"

"One of Satan's many faults and sins is that he takes without giving. Takes without asking. Them apples is left out to find Satan. Traveler comes through and don't take the apples, he's as godly as the Ancients think an outsider can be. Traveler comes through and takes the apples…"

"He's Satan," I said.

"Bingo," Ike said stuffing eggs and fried potatoes with wild onions in his mouth.

"But we didn't know…"

"Don't matter," Ike said chewing his food. "Knowing ain't the point. The point is you took them apples out of greed and selfishness. Now, I personally don't see a whole lot wrong with that. Greed and selfishness is 'bout the best survival skill you'll ever acquire, but the Ancients don't feel the way I do."

Miss Connie started piling food on my plate. "No need to fill the boy with stories."

"It ain't stories. It's real. I knew a fella that done the same. Ancients cut him up into pieces and scattered him all about the pass. Their dogs left nothing but bones."

"Ike Decker!" Miss Connie shot him a look that could turn a charging horse away.

"It's the truth. Skinny fella named Robbins lived about twenty miles East of here."

I held a piece of bacon but couldn't bring myself to eat it. "We just won't go through the pass again. We'll go around."

Ike gulped some coffee. "Boy, the Ancients don't come out of the pass but for one thing."

"What?" I asked even though I was more than sure I wouldn't like the answer.

"To hunt down Satan."

***

I struggled to eat. I hated passing on food of any kind, much less the good eats that Ike was offering up, but his story about the Ancients got to me. I felt like most of what he said was just to get my back up, but that didn't prevent me from losing my appetite and feeling madder than hell at Doreen.

When you get right down to it, she's the one who got them apples. I didn't even know they were there. She climbed up the rocks and brung'em down. Not me. As far as I was concerned, she was to blame. I didn't have much to do with it at all if you really thought about it. I mean I did eat a couple, but I only did that because they were in Doreen's possession. I stepped into the picture after the transaction of taking them had already taken place. If the Ancients ever come hunting me down, I'd tell them exactly that, too. I wasn't going to be cut up into little pieces and thrown about the pass for no girl, not a mute barren girl for sure.

I sat on the front porch with Ike while he smoked one of his smelly cigarettes. Doreen and Miss Connie was strolling through the property studying the tiny white flowers that was scattered about. Of course, Bob was following them around like he was their pet. Doreen had won his heart with her belly rubbing and scrap feeding.

Ike talked while he held in some smoke. "That Connie cuts the figure, don't she?"

I shrugged.

He let out a long breath. "No, I mean it. Got generous curves. Nice hips. Got a sweet little slope there in the small of her back, too. I like that slope."

"You do?"

"Sure. You don't?"

"Never thought about a girl's slopes."

He pointed at me with the cigarette pinched between his finger and thumb. "You a breast man?"

I recoiled like a snake. "I ain't no kind of man."

He nodded. "That's a good point. Well, let me mold your female preferences for ya'. Breasts are the silk of a woman. They look nice, feel good, fun to run your fingers across, but they ain't durable. The wear down and sag. Same with the ass, too. Lot of men go for the heart-shaped ass that sets up and jiggles when a woman walks. Stays nice for awhile, but it drops."

"Drops?"

"Like a stone off a mountain. A man who falls for the ass and/or tits of a woman is going to wake up sadly disappointed one day. It's an inevitability. Now, mind you, I'm talking 'bout the woman you're to marry. If you're looking for a gal to roll around with for a short time, shop for the best silk you can get. But for the woman you're going to bury your forever into, shop for the woman who's got granite."

"And that's the slopes?"

He sucked on his cigarette. "That it is, my boy. Slopes don't give into age. Slopes is the frame. They're what's known as the sensual part of a woman. It's where nature took extra care to piece the female form together." He smiled.

I shook my head. "I think those cigarettes rattle your thinking."

"That they do," a voice said coming from behind Ike.

We were both dumbfounded to see Abel standing there. Even though we were elevated on the porch, he met us eyelevel.

"Abel," Ike said.

Abel nodded hello.

I stared with my mouth hanging open, although I was unaware of it at the time.

"Running low of drink," Abel said.

"Got some rye whiskey in cold storage," Ike said.

"Don't do well with rye. No corn liquor?"

"Might have a bottle."

"That's hardly enough."

"All I got for now. I can travel over to the Anderson's and see if they got some."

Abel snorted. "Might as well pour poison down my throat. More kerosene than liquor."

"It's all I can offer for now."

There was nothing said for what felt like a couple of minutes.

Ike finally said, "You give the boy's offer any more thought?"

"What offer?"

"What we talked about yesterday. The town... the marauders... the rector who sent the boy to hire you for your services..."

"That. I was half in the bag when we talked."

"You want me to go over it again?"

"What're you, the kid's agent? You got some kind of stake in his proposal?"

Abel shook his head. "It ain't a stake exactly. I do figure on reaping some of the pay."

"You the one they send for?"

"No, but I aim to lend my assistance. I mean we are brothers."

"We got the same father. That just makes us half brothers."

Ike smiled. "And I don't expect more than half the pay."

Abel peered around Ike and looked at me. "I'll take the rye."

"What?"

"You said you had rye. I'll take some."

"But what about the boy's offer?"

"Get me the rye, and I'll think it over."

Ike hesitated and then stood. He clomped around me and into the house, mumbling to himself the whole way.

I sat nervously as Abel refused to take his eyes off me. I tried not to make eye contact with him, but I slipped every once in awhile and caught a glimpse of his horrible hateful face.

"You an expert at hiring killers?" Abel asked after torturing me with his stares for more than a few minutes.

"No, sir?"

"Why'd they send you?"

"Because we was the only ones that had a horse?"

"I didn't see you ride in on a horse."

"Had to shoot it with my Pa's army issue. Broke its leg in Besser Pass."

"Army issue? Your Pa was in the war?"

"Yes, sir. 'Fore I was born."

"Why didn't he come out here to talk to me?"

"Broke his back in the war. He can't ride. Only trusted me with the horse."

"And you shot it?"

"Yes, sir."

"What's his name?"

"John Arnaught."

Abel studied the name.

"You know him?' I asked.

He shook his head. "Never heard of him."

Ike stepped out of the house with a wood box full of bottles of rye whiskey. He handed it to Abel.

Abel took it and scanned the box. "Store bought."

"Got'em from a place in Crowder."

"Crowder's a shit hole."

"Most places are these days, Abel."

The giant for a man nodded. He turned to leave, but stopped and looked back. "I'll be eating dinner with you tonight."

Ike was shocked. "You will?"

"We'll discuss the boy's business."

I felt scared and hopeful all at once.

"I'll go out with Bob and bring back fresh boar."

Abel shook his head as he walked away. "Fucking bear's going to eat you one of these days."

***

As promised, Ike hunted down a boar and prepared it for dinner. He split the bounty with Bob, who disappeared into the woods with his half of the four hundred pound pig. Ike cooked our half over a spit in the back of the house.

Miss Connie and Doreen threw together the sides from the supplies in cold storage. By the time we sat down to eat, we had us a regular feast.

Barely a word was spoke throughout the meal. Abel stared at his plate the entire time. He ate three times as much as the rest of us, probably because he was bigger than all four of us combined. He didn't have no use for a napkin, and wasn't that swift with a knife and fork. I ain't never seen a body eat the way he did. I reckon it would have been less offensive to find Bob in the woods and watch him tear his half of the boar from the bone.

When Abel shoveled the last mound of food into his mouth, he pushed back and belched. "What's the pay?"

I looked at Ike and waited for him to answer, but he indicated with a nod that I should do the talking.

"Ike agreed on two of our women."

Abel sucked food out of his teeth. "Women?"

"Yes, sir. Of your choosing, of course."

He stood and walked to the counter where there were three bottles of rye. "My choosing? How do the women of your town feel about this arrangement?"

I shrugged. "Don't know. I reckon they'll go along with it because Old Kelly will see to it."

He picked up a bottle and opened it. "Old Kelly?"

"Our rector."

He took a drink. "Man or woman?"

"Woman."

"And she runs things in Two Notch?"

"Yes, sir."

He sat back down with the bottle in hand. "What if I was to choose this Old Kelly as one of the women?"

I crinkled my nose in disgust. "Can't see why you'd want to do something like that."

"Why not? She's a woman ain't she?"

"Yes, sir, but there's a reason we call her Old Kelly."

He took another drink. "Old make you worthless, does it?"

I thought about the question. "No, sir. Not in everyday living, but I reckon it lessens your value a might as a good trade in services."

"So, you're saying Old Kelly is off the table?"

"Not exactly, I'm just saying you wouldn't want her on the table. She ain't just old. She's barely tolerable to be around."

He twirled the bottle around and watched the brown liquid swirl. "You just described me, boy."

"I reckon that's true," I said without thinking.

He looked at me hard at first and then gave a half smile. "I ain't one for trading in human beings. Got no moral objection to the practice. I just don't like people enough to trade for 'em."

"I ain't got the authority to go beyond three women."

"Three?" Ike said.

"I'll do it for a hat full of gold."

"You heard the boy, Abel. He ain't got the authority to deal in anything but female companions."

"Old Kelly will take the deal."

"How do you know?" I asked.

"Because people always give me what I want."

I thought it over. "What kind of hat?"

He gave me a full grin this time. "I'll supply the hat."

"How 'bout the gold and the women?" Ike asked

Abel stood.

"A woman?

Abel picked up the bottle. "We leave in the morning. We got four horses and two saddles. I don't subscribe to that gentleman bullshit, so I get one of the saddles. And I'm leaving it up to my fat-ass brother on whether to take the other one for himself or bequeath it to you ladies."

Miss Connie sneered. "We ladies can ride without a saddle."

"I doubt it," Abel said walking away from the table.

"Abel," Ike shouted. "I ain't going if I don't get a lady companion out of the deal."

"Don't go," Abel said exiting the house.

Ike slammed his open hand on the table. "Damn it! You don't never give me a thought. Not a single solitary thought!" He gritted his teeth. "Okay, I'll go!"

Miss Connie covered her mouth to conceal her amusement at his helplessness.

"I'll just court a lady when I get there. Gotta be at least one that wants to leave that shithole for a town. Right?"

Miss Connie snorted out a laugh.

"Go ahead laugh. I'll be laughing tomorrow once your ample ass does about an hour on one of them horses."

The wind howled through the Decker brothers' valley that night. The strength of it bent and twisted tree limbs so far they creaked as if they would snap in half at any moment. The moon hovered over the tree tops peeking behind fast moving clouds. Dancing shadows floated through the windows of Ike's house and decorated the walls. It was enough to drive a body crazy.

I gave up the notion that I could sleep a room away from Miss Connie and Doreen. I huddled up next to them as soon as they drifted off to sleep. They were none the wiser which meant I could hold onto my dignity at least one more day by not having to admit I was a scared little kid.

I dozed off at some point. It was a state that snuck up on me. I expected to be awake all night listening to this sound and that. Watching the shadows turn into creatures out to get me. But sleep dropped down on me and smothered me into bliss.

Can't say how long I was out before I was snapped to by a noise that sounded like footsteps. Against all my wants, I lifted my head and surveyed the room, and about lost my supper when I seen a small figure standing at the window with its back to me. I swallowed and lifted myself up on my elbows to get a better look. It was Doreen.

Careful not to wake Miss Connie, I got up and joined the little mute girl.

"Whatcha doing, Doreen?"

She didn't answer. She kept her focus on the world outside.

"You ought not be sneaking around here at night. Might scare Miss Connie. That ain't nice at all."

She turned to me and snickered. She knew I was protesting for me more than Miss Connie.

"Whatcha locked onto out there?"

She raised a finger and pressed it against the glass.

I followed the direction she was pointing to and scanned the woods. I couldn't make out nothing but dancing trees. I wiped away some dust on the window and leaned forward. "Can't hardly see nothing..." My heart jumped when I seen two green orbs dash from one tree to another. Then a second set of the lantern eyes appeared and a third. There must've been a half dozen pair of them out there.

My mouth went dry and my hands begun to shake. "They come for Satan."

Doreen didn't do nothing but shrug. I couldn't understand how she could be so calm about it. The lantern eyes was here. They come out of the pass and was on our trail. And, they weren't just after me. They were after her, too. She was the one. She took the damn apples. I turned halfway to her when I seen the amber glow of Abel's pipe coming from his porch. He sat staring right at the green glowing eyes.

I breathed a little easier. It didn't matter how many of them lantern eyes was out there, they wouldn't dare advance on us with Abel Decker on the job. He was a hell of a lot more terrifying than chasing down Satan.

I grabbed Doreen by the shoulders and pulled her away from the window. "Let's not tempt em. Let Abel handle it."

She walked like a zombie back to Miss Connie and took her spot on the floor. I give Abel and the lantern eyes one more look before I did the same. Doreen was asleep before I set down.

Abel Decker was almost too drunk to take his mount in the morning. He took aim with his foot on the stirrup four times before he found it. Ike sat on his horse like a fat tick wearing a ridiculously big hat and laughed at his brother's silliness the whole time.

Once Abel was atop his horse, he turned his head to the right and threw up all over the rump of the horse Miss Connie and Doreen was to ride. The horse lurched forward and then whinnied in protest. The whole scene set Ike off to laughing harder. It was a sad, poor sight, and I lost a little bit of my confidence in Abel Decker's hire.

"Goddamn horse is crooked," Abel said with more slur and spit than I've seen come out of a man.

"I need a towel or rag to wipe this disgusting mess off the back of my horse," Miss Connie said.

"Ain't got time for cleanliness," Abel said. "Climb atop the fucking thing and let's go."

"I will not," Miss Connie said.

I guided my horse over to her. "Here take my mount."

"No," Abel said. "She'll ride the horse I assigned her or she'll walk."

"It don't make no difference to me," I said.

"It does to me. I'm in command. If my orders don't hold before we even leave my property, there ain't much hope for the rest of the trip."

"Command?' Miss Connie said. "You're not in command. You're the employee here, Mr. Abel Decker. If anyone is in command, it's the boy."

Abel's face pinched in. "The boy?" He reached inside his jacket, pulled out a pistol, and pointed it at me. "You in command, boy?"

I stepped back with my hands raised. "Me, sir? No, sir?"

He moved his sights from me to something just behind me. I turned to see Doreen cocking her arm back ready to bean a rock at Abel's head. "I'll put a hole in your head before that rock leaves your hand, little girl."

Miss Connie stepped in front of her. "What kind of man threatens a child?"

"A man who's put down a few in his day."

We all stood in the shadow of what he said and let the shock of it wear off. I grabbed the mane of my horse and somehow managed to climb on its back with my Pa's army issue strapped around my shoulder and my backpack on. "No need to shoot nobody, Mr. Decker. You're in command." I shifted the horse around. "He's in command, Doreen. Drop the rock."

She did as I said, and I turned the horse back to him. He held the gun a moment or two longer and then replaced it back underneath his coat.

Miss Connie helped Doreen up on the back of their horse and then climbed up herself, stoically sitting in Abel's puke.

He donned a satisfied sneer and pulled his hat down to shade his eyes.

"That ain't much of a hat to fill with gold," I said.

He kicked his horse and started toward the tree line. "This ain't the hat for gold." He pointed over his shoulder at Ike. "That is."

Ike frowned under the brim of his ten-gallon cowboy hat.

The horses lined up in a row with Abel's black steed taking the lead. My blonde horse with black mane and tail come second followed by Connie and Doreen's black and white pony. Ike's powder gray mare brought up the rear. Bob shadowed us. He'd show himself from time to time, but mostly he kept out of sight.

The path wasn't much of a path at all. I got a tree limb to the face about every five minutes. It didn't help that Abel's broad build would push the limbs to their optimal bounce back position. It was like I was getting whipped about my cheeks and forehead.

Abel tilted his whiskey bottle about as often as I got smacked in the face. Apparently, starting the trip drunk wasn't enough drunk for him. He'd finish a bottle, reach in his saddleback and retrieve a fresh one. For a man who didn't care much for rye, he drank a hell of a lot of it.

"Your daddy broke his back in the war, did he?" The question fell out his mouth caked in whiskey soaked saliva. He did a half turn and I could see a string of drool hanging from the corner of his mouth.

"Yes, sir. He did."

"Hell of thing, that is. Used to be a thing like that would leave a man permanently unabled."

"Yes, sir."

"Fucking field doctors morphine a kid up with a broke back and ship him home with an expiration tag. You know what I mean?"

"No, sir. I'm afraid I don't."

He took a swig of rye. "They didn't fix the fucking pain. Masked it with drugs. Didn't give a shit if he lived or died."

I didn't reply. I wasn't sure he was really talking to me. I think he was talking because the whiskey had set his tongue to wagging.

"But about year twelve of the war healthy young fuckers was in short supply. They were running out of people to fight their goddamn war. Can't have that, can we?"

I kept tight lipped.

"You listening to me, boy?"

"Yes, sir,"

"Well answer when a man directs a question to you."

"Yes, sir. I suppose you can't have a war if there ain't nobody to do the fighting."

"Damn right." He drank and then wiped his mouth with his sleeve. "The sonny-bitch doctors suddenly come up with a way to fix most broken backs, broken bones, broken skulls. Basically, if it was broke, they found a way to fix it and fix it fast. Young person come in with a broken body part, they could have the soldier up and out the door in 48 hours. I don't know what the fuck they come up with, but they did it because you can't have a war without fuckers to do all your killing and dying."

"Yes, sir."

"But your daddy must have been really fubar because they got him walking and sent him home."

"He's pert near a cripple though. Can't stay on his feet too long. Aches him something awful. He ain't had more than a couple of hours of sleep in a stretch since I can remember."

"Hell, ain't no soldier worth his salt able to sleep more than a couple of hours at a time. If you ain't haunted by the things you seen and done, you ain't right in the head."

"You haunted?"

He downed the rest of the bottle and tossed it aside. "Hell, no, but son, I definitely ain't right in the head.

Abel bent over to grab another bottle out of his saddlebag, but stopped short. He held up his hand and brought the train of horses to a halt. He scanned the woods in front of us. "Where's that damn bear of yours, Ike?"

"Saw him about a click back snoozing under a fir." By the sound of his voice, it was obvious he was stirring out of a sleep. "Why?"

Abel slowly reached inside his coat and retrieved his pistol. I ducked my head underneath the strap of my Pa's gun and rested it across my lap. "We in for trouble?"

"We are."

"What is it?" Ike asked.

"Hear something?"

"We're in the woods," Miss Connie said. "If you didn't hear anything, I'd question your hearing. There's no need to go jumping at every little noise."

We heard the tell-tale sound of a firearm cocking. "Well put, lady."

We all turned to the voice and seen a man with one arm freshly cut off at the elbow, and a gun in his remaining hand. He was descending the woods to our right with his gun trained on Doreen's head.

"Don't get no ideas, any of you. I may look beat and undone, but I promise you I can part this little girl's hair with one bullet and put a second one right through her eye."

His face was pale and appeared to be losing color as he stood before us, and he was drenched in blood. He fluttered his eyelashes a few times as he was fighting off the urge to pass out.

"You couldn't hit a barn with a scatter gun," Abel said.

"Don't try my mind, mister. I'm a desperate man with shooting skills you ain't never dreamed of."

"Well, there's a barrel of truth for ya'." Abel said. "I never wasted a minute dreaming about your skills, shooting or otherwise." He hiccupped and laughed.

"I'm warning you, old man. I will kill this girl." The desperation he spoke of was coming through loud and clear in the timbre of his voice.

"What do you want?" Miss Connie asked.

"Don't make a damn what he wants," Abel said. "He ain't getting nothing but a bullet knocking out his teeth."

Miss Connie practically growled. "I believe this gentleman has the drop on us, Mr. Decker. Thanks to your drinking skills."

"What are saying? This is my fault?"

"You are in command, aren't you? There's a half-witted one-armed marksman holding a gun on Doreen in the middle of the woods, isn't there?"

"Decker?' The man said. "Abel Decker?"

"None of your business," Abel said.

"The one and only," Miss Connie said.

"Shut your flap, whore."

"Don't call me that!"

"Why not? Ike says that's what you are!"

"But I said she was on holiday," Ike said.

"Shut up!" the one-armed bandit said.

The bickering came to a stop.

"Now, with all due reverence to the great Abel Decker and to the vacationing whore, I'm afraid I'm going to have to ask you all to climb down off those horses."

"All of us?" Ike asked.

"That's what I said?"

"You robbing us?" I asked.

"I'm taking your horses and whatever supplies will get me to Clinton."

"All our horses?" Ike asked.

"All."

"But you ain't got but one ass to sit on and ride."

"Don't want you following me."

"We won't follow you. Swear it," Ike said.

"Everyone shut your damn mouths," Abel said swaying in his saddle. "Mister, you ain't getting these horses, not four, not three, not one. You understand me?"

"I understand, but that ain't the way it's going to be."

"You know who I am, right?"

"Yes, indeed I do. I served in the 106th with you on a tour."

Abel peered at him. "Is that right?"

"It is. Seen you do things a man shouldn't be able to do."

Abel winked. "I was good at my job."

"Well," the one-armed bandit said, "I wouldn't say you was so much good as you was depraved. When I say shouldn't, I ain't talking about your physical ability. I mean you dashed just about every idea of morality that I ever seen. I ain't sure how you was able to let your mind talk you into doing some of the things you done."

Abel scowled. "Told you, I was good at my job."

"That may be the case, and frankly, knowing who you are now, I've come to the notion that me training a pistol at this little girl's head as a deterrent ain't going to have the desired effect in the end."

"You've got the right notion, soldier."

The man grimaced. "I'd just assume you not call me that." His hand started to shake.

"Fair enough," Abel said lifting up in his saddle.

"Don't move, Mr. Decker. I won't shoot the girl, but I'll shoot you."

"Son, I'm going to climb down off this horse and shoot you point blank between the eyes, and you ain't going to do a thing about it."

"What are you doing, Abel?" Ike asked.

"Like the lady said, I got the drop on you."

"You got the drop on me, true, but not on my fat-ass brother's bear friend."

"Bear friend?"

Just as the words left the one-armed bandit's mouth, Bob emerged from a row of brush behind him and pounced. He sank his teeth into the fleshy part of his shoulder and yanked him to the ground. We could hear the bone snap. The poor man screamed. His good arm was rendered useless.

"Call him off," Miss Connie said. "Call him off, please!" She shielded her eyes with her hands.

I couldn't look away. Bob was chewing on a piece of meat he had ripped from the man, and I was so horrified I was fascinated to no end.

Ike whistled and Bob stepped back right away. A trained dog couldn't have been more obedient.

I turned to see what Abel's reaction was to the attack, and seen him slumped over. He was snoring up a storm. His drink had finally gotten to him. We all watched as he leaned farther and farther to the right until he fell with a thud to the forest floor.

***

The fall didn't break his neck, but it didn't rouse him either. He just curled up and kept on snoozing away. We wasn't going nowhere for awhile.

Miss Connie barked out orders to all of us once it was clear Abel wasn't in any condition to object. She told Ike to get his damn bear as far away from us as possible. Once Bob was out of sight, she jumped off her horse and tended to the one-armed bandit.

He was in a dying condition. There wasn't nothing to be done for him, but that didn't stop Miss Connie. She took some of our water supply and cleaned his wounds best she could. Doreen set a blanket out for him, and me and Ike done our best to lay him on it without causing him more pain than necessary. The missing hand didn't seem to bother him as much as the bear bite and freshly broken bone. The stump did have a powerful odor that set all our eyes to watering.

"Oh, man," the bandit said as he sobbed. "There weren't no call to get the bear involved. It just weren't necessary at all."

Ike raised an eyebrow. "Pretty high minded talk coming from a guy who had a gun aimed at a little girl's head."

"I was bluffing, goddamn it!"

"Take it easy," Miss Connie said. "What's done is done."

"I'm a dead man. That's what's done!"

She wiped the dirt from his forehead. "I hate to tell you this, but the smell coming from that stump of yours indicates that you were dying before Bob intervened."

"Who the hell is Bob?"

"The bear."

He giggled. "That's just great. I've been killed by a bear named Bob."

"You were killed by your own stupidity," Ike said.

"I was desperate. You think I'm stupid. I got a nose. I can smell. I know I got a blood sickness, but I figured I still had enough time to make it to Clinton by horse and get it tended to."

"How'd you get your hand cut off in the first place I asked?"

He groaned. "Fucking marauders."

I pert near swallowed my tongue when I heard those words come out his mouth. Old Kelly did have a vision. The fucking marauders was real. The silence coming from the others told me they were thinking the same thing.

"Bastards swooped down on me near Besser Pass. Took my horse. Took my supplies. Took my hand. Left me with the clothes on my back and the gun I hide in my boot."

"How many of them were there?" Ike asked.

"Twelve, maybe fifteen. Lead by an ugly cuss named Theodore Harding. Man had more scar than face."

"Harding?" Ike said falling back on his fat ass. "I'll be damned."

"You know him?" Miss Connie asked.

"Heard of him. He's ransacked just about every town in these parts. Left all them bloody and broken. Takes the young'uns and trades them to the military for gold and weapons."

"And he's meaner than Abel Decker by a country mile," the one-arm bandit said.

"Then the war ain't over?" I asked.

Ike pulled one of his cigarettes from his shirt pocket. "Let's just say it's on hold because everyone run out of soldiers. Harding's helping out that cause, though. His own personal conscription service. Heard rumors the military is preparing to send kids younger than your mute girl into battle. Thought they was just rumors 'til now."

"That's madness," Miss Connie said.

Ike lit his cigarette. "World went insane decades ago."

The one-armed bandit let out a scream. "Lord just take me! I'm hurting too bad!"

Ike took the cigarette and held it to the stranger's mouth. "Take a drag."

"I don't smoke."

"It's for the pain."

The stranger hesitated and then tilted his head toward the cigarette. He grimaced and then sucked in some of the smoke, causing him to cough and growl in pain.

"Jesus, you can't jump in so deep if you ain't never smoked before," Ike said. "Draw it in slow."

The stranger did as Ike instructed and took in some smoke and held it. He actually appeared to relax as he let it out.

"There, see? It calls in a soothing underneath, don't it?"

The stranger nodded and took another drag with Ike's help.

"What do you know?" Miss Connie asked. "You're not as worthless as I thought, Ike."

"Miss Connie," he said, "if it's one thing I know, it's my special smokes. Been growing the plants for near twenty years now. Smoking them longer than that."

The stranger smiled. "I'd thank you, but as I recall, it was your bear friend that got me in this condition."

Ike brought the cigarette to his mouth and took a drag. "Yeah, well Bob's a complicated individual."

The stranger's eyelids got heavier and heavier. "Name's Austin Clark, by the way... I think. Wait... no, that's right. That's my name." He laughed with a worried look on his face.

Ike slapped his leg and laughed. "That's the smoke. It makes you question everything that comes out of your mouth."

I wished I could feel as diminished as they were feeling. If Harding and his men met up with Austin at Besser Pass that meant they were on their way to Two Notch. They weren't but two days away when they took his hand. "How long ago did you have your run in with Harding and his men?"

Austin gave me a droopy stare. "Two days ago... I think. No, it was just a day ago. Had to be."

"They say where they were headed?"

"We didn't exactly go over our social calendars," he said with a giggle. "They left me for dead."

"They say anything about Two Notch?"

"Two Notch?" Austin gave my question some thought. "You know, I think they did. They had some dealings there. Yeah, they did. They were late for a meet up with a fella named Buster."

"Buster?" The name sent chills up my spine.

"Pretty sure he was waiting for them on the other side of the pass."

I looked at Doreen and I could tell she was thinking the same thing I was. We should have killed Buster when we had the chance.

***

The night brought the coolest temperatures yet. The wind picked up and my teeth took to chattering. Ike built a fire, but it didn't hardly help none. Miss Connie and Doreen huddled next to each other and sat with the bottoms of their shoes exposed to the flame.

Austin Clark was drifting out of this world fast. He'd mumble and cough from time to time, but for the most part he just moaned into the darkness. A body couldn't help but feel bad for him and also be annoyed by him. He was just lingering and grating on our nerves with his declining state.

Abel come to the minute we opened a can of beans for supper. He pushed himself up to a sitting position and stared at the fire without saying word one for near ten minutes. When he finally did speak, it wasn't a positive experience.

"Fucking moaning and bitching is grinding me. Why ain't you killed him yet?"

Ike shoveled a spoonful of beans into his mouth. "Seemed redundant given that he probably ain't gonna make it 'til morning."

"Christ, if he ain't irritating as piss though."

"Your compassion for your fellow man is startling, Abel Decker," Miss Connie said without giving him the courtesy of making eye contact with him.

"The compassionate thing to do would be to put the poor bastard out of his misery."

"Considered that," Ike said. "But he's giving us some good intel on these marauders we're to come up against. I thought it might do some good to see if he's got anything else worthwhile to share."

Miss Connie shook her head. "I see you Decker boys have the same level of give-a-shit in your bleak hearts."

"He's mumbling gibberish," Abel said, ignoring her. "He ain't got nothing useful left to say."

Ike scooped up more beans. "You kill him then."

Abel waved him off. "Too tired to trust my aim. Liable to blow his ear off and have to hear him bitch and moan even more."

"Disgusting," Miss Connie said.

"What was his intel?"

"Theodore Harding and his boys is who we're going up against."

Abel struggled to stand. "That name supposed to mean something?" He stumbled to his horse and propped himself up with a hand on its rump. With his other hand, he unzipped his fly and pulled his pecker out.

"What are you doing?" Miss Connie said, covering Doreen's eyes.

"Pissing."

"Do you have to do it right here?"

"I could come closer if you want," he said with a throaty laugh.

"Good Lord!"

He kept on about his business. "What about this Theodore Harding?"

"He's meaner than you," I said before Ike could jump in. "That's what Austin says anyway."

"Who's Austin?"

"The one-armed fella that Bob bit," I said pointing at the poor miserable wretch dying on one of our blankets.

"Oh." Abel zipped up his pants and went for the saddlebag. "Well, if this fella wants to be meaner than me, he can be meaner than me. I ain't lobbying for the title." He pulled a cloth bag of coffee out of his saddlebag. I was surprised it wasn't a bottle of rye.

"He's probably in Two Notch by now," I said.

Abel returned fireside with the coffee, a small tin pot and some water. He poured the water in the pot and placed it close to the fire without setting it in it. "He ain't in no hurry to leave."

"What makes you say that?" I asked.

"Because there ain't no law in Two Notch from what I hear. None to speak of anyway. He'll let his men have their way with the town and the folks in it for a week or two. Kind of a re-ward of sorts."

"How do you know so much about a man you've never heard of?' Miss Connie asked.

"Two reasons. One, I know fucking marauders. I've run across and with them for more years than you've even thought about going boots up with strangers for pay. And two, if this Harding is as mean as me, that means he'd do what I'd do."

"Not mean as," Ike said. "Meaner than."

"Whatever. The point is we got plenty of time to catch and kill these assholes."

"Not before they use Two Notch up," I said.

"No big loss from what I here," Abel said.

"Go to hell, Abel Decker," I said. "Go to hell on a rocket sled!" I didn't know what a rocket sled was, but I'd heard a couple of the old folks in town use the term and it seemed to fit just right for this occasion. He may not have given a shit about Two Notch, but I did. It wasn't the town so much as it was some of the folks. The few good ones there were. And when you get down to it, that's mostly what a town worth saving is, good folks.

Abel laughed. "Well, well. The soldier's back may be broken, but there ain't nothing wrong with his boy's." He stuck his finger in the water in the pot and twirled it around. "Five more minutes."

I kicked the pot and tipped it into the fire, dousing the flames on one log.

Abel hooked his meaty hands around the back of my neck and yanked me over to him. "Boy, don't fuck with my coffee."

I was close to letting the tears fly. I was scared as shit.

"Let him go," Miss Connie said jumping to her feet.

"Boy's got to learn to respect his elders."

"And you got to learn that filthy old drunks that threaten children don't deserve respect."

Ike appeared as scared as I was. I figured right away that didn't bode well for me 'cause he must've seen his brother all kinds of mad before. He knew better than anybody what state moved Abel to do terrible things.

Abel stood and picked me up with him. He twirled me around and held me by my coat collar. "I'm going to toss you in the fire so you can fetch my little tin pot."

"Stop!" Miss Connie said.

"Stay out of this!"

She turned to Ike. "Stop him!"

Ike didn't move.

Out of the corner of my eye, I seen Doreen pick up a rock. I shook my head and gestured for her to drop it. Thank God Abel didn't notice.

"You ain't gotta throw me in," I said. "I'll fetch it on my own."

"I'd rather toss you in." He was lifting me up higher and higher. It wasn't long before we was nose to nose.

I heard a yelp.

"Fuck all… shit!"

It was Ike. He was pulling the tin pot out of the fire.

"Here's your goddamn pot, Abel!" He shook his hand and it tumbled to the ground next to Abel's feet.

Abel looked down at the pot and then back at me. "Pick it up."

"You're going to have to leave me go," I said.

He planted me back on the ground. "Pick it up with your bare hands and heat me up some more water for my coffee."

"He'll burn his hands," Miss Connie said.

"He goes in the fire or he does as I say."

"It's okay, Miss Connie." I quickly reached down and picked up the cup before I could talk myself out of it. It sent sharp, shooting pains through my whole hand.

Abel waited for the pain to become too much. He waited for me to drop it and cry like a baby. I gritted my teeth and squeezed the pot harder. There was no way I was letting go.

He sat back down and said, "Get on with it."

***

Abel the bastard took watch while the rest of us slept. Sleeping was the last thing I wanted to do. We'd only traveled about a mile and half from the Decker brother's property, and I was more than sure Harding was having his way with Two Notch. If I had my druthers, we'd be on horseback moving our way towards my hometown.

But neither Abel nor Miss Connie shared my druthers. Abel was hung over like the drunk son-of-a-bitch he was. Travel was the last thing he wanted to undertake. Miss Connie didn't want to leave the dying man's side. There weren't a lick of hope for him, but she just couldn't leave him.

I slept curled up next to my Pa's army issue. I wasn't so much worried about intruders as I was about Abel. I knew it wasn't no idle threat he made when he said he was going to toss me in the fire. He meant it and was a breath away from doing it when Ike stepped in. There wasn't a chance in hell I was going to leave myself defenseless in the company of Abel Decker ever again.

Doreen slept next to Miss Connie. She seemed to sleep without a care in the world. If she was simple like people said, I'd like to try it out for myself. Nothing seemed to frazzle her.

Miss Connie fell asleep with her head on her knees sitting next to Austin Clark and as far as I know, didn't stir a bit. She held a wet rag in her hand that dried out before the moon started dropping out of the sky.

Ike snored away with his ten gallon hat over his face. His bulbous belly inflated and deflated with every log he sawed in his sleep. It jolted me out of my light slumber more than once, and I understood how a man could get shot for snoring too loud.

On one occasion, Ike snorted and I woke biting my lip. I lifted my head to shoot him dirty looks, but quickly diverted my attention to Abel. He wasn't in his original spot. He'd moved over near Austin Clark and was on one knee next to him. I seen the wounded man's feet twitch. The flames of the fire bent in their direction, and I seen why Abel had taken an interest in the man. He was covering Austin's mouth and nose with his giant hand, smothering him to death.

I raised up and thought about yelling out, but I stopped myself. I had two reasons. My stinging palms served as a reminder of what kind of pain Abel Decker was capable of inflicting on another human being without even laying a finger on him. The bastard scared the shit out of me. I wanted to avoid another run in with him at all costs.

Second, I'm ashamed to admit it, but I wanted the man to die. If he was still alive in the morning, Miss Connie would insist on staying to take care of him. She'd probably tell us to go on without her, and there wasn't no part of me that wanted to be left in the company of just Abel and Ike without her. She was a likable whore that just made me feel more at ease.

Abel caught me taking the scene in, and he actually smiled at me. The bastard wore a hateful frown doing everyday things, but killing another man put a god-awful smile on his face.

I laid back down and closed my eyes. For reasons I don't care to know about, I didn't have no trouble falling back to sleep.

I woke up a short time later to a twig snapping. Raising up, I seen Abel back in his original spot, but turned away from the fire. He was facing something in the woods. I looked past him and seen a row of lantern eyes through the brush in the distance staring back at us.

I crawled over to Abel.

He looked down at me. "They come for you, boy."

I swallowed.

"Don't worry. I'll keep them at bay."

I felt a swell of relief come over me. They outnumbered him by a good bit, but I didn't have no doubts he could handle them. I don't know why exactly. He just had a way of making you feel that not even God himself could take down Abel Decker in a fight. I wasn't sure why he wanted to protect me. He made it clear that he didn't think much of me.

"I figure I gotta bring you back alive to Two Notch in order to make my case for the renegotiating of the payment terms." He gave me a hard look. "Alive don't mean in one piece, so don't get any ideas that I've had a change of heart about you."

I crawled back to my spot and said, "I ain't got no idea you even got a heart."

He snickered.

***

Morning came and Abel woke us by kicking Ike in the ass. The fat bearded man yelled like he'd been shot with a cannon.

"Goddamn, Abel!"

"We need to get on the move."

"You could have just tapped me on the shoulder or give me a good shake. That ain't no way to wake a man."

"It worked," Abel said hoisting his saddle on his horse's back.

"I'm not going," Miss Connie said as she roused.

"Why?" I asked.

"Someone's got to look after Mr. Clark. We can't just leave…" She looked at the dead man.

"Dead men don't need looking after," Abel said. He pulled the strap on the saddle taut and glared at me.

I bit my lip to keep from talking

If she suspected Abel had done the poor man in, she didn't say anything. "We at least have to bury him."

"We don't."

"Miss Connie's right. We should do that much," I said.

"We shouldn't."

"We're just going to leave him here?" Miss Connie said. "Out in the open?"

"We are."

"We can't do that…"

"Oh, for Christ's sake!" Abel said as he turned to us red faced. "The man is dead. D-E-A-D! That means what's left there is meat and bones and organs. In fact…" He stomped over to Austin, reached down and grabbed the man by the collar, and dragged the body out into a small clearing. "Call your bear, Ike."

Ike was stumbling to his feet when his brother made the request. "What?"

"Your bear. Call your goddamn bear!"

"You wouldn't," Miss Connie said to Abel. "That's even too inhuman for you."

"It's the cycle of life," Abel said.

"Abel, you can't expect me to do a thing like that."

Abel walked up on his brother and grimaced. "Call your bear over here. Let's not let the man's death go to waste."

Ike stroked his beard and stepped back. He moved his eyes from Abel and turned to Miss Connie. "It is just meat when you get down to it."

"Goddamn you, Ike Decker. It's a person."

"Was a person," Ike said. "If Bob don't eat him, there will be a dozen scavengers that will move in as soon as we leave."

"We should bury him," Miss Connie said as sternly as she could.

"And what do you think will happen to him when we bury him?" Abel asked. "He's still meat underground. The worms will get to him. Bugs, moles, rats, you name it, there's plenty of underground beasties that will get their fill of old Austin Clark."

Miss Connie turned her attention to me. "Am I alone in this?"

I looked down and kicked the ground. "He ain't wrong, Miss Connie. He's just as much food underground as he is above."

Her shoulders dropped like someone had taken all of the air out of her. "I see." She grabbed Doreen's hand and led her to their horse. "Do it then, but at least have the decency to let me get the girl out of the area first."

"You've got two minutes," Abel said as he walked back to his horse.

Ike scratched his beard and yawned. "Nothing like light conversations about death and body disposal to start your morning."

I approached him and whispered, "He killed him." I don't know what possessed me to say it. I guess holding the secret in was just eating at me.

"What?"

"Abel killed Mr. Clark. I seen it with my own eyes last night."

Ike put a hand on my shoulder. "Forget you saw it."

"I don't know if I can."

"Listen, the man was going to die anyway. Abel saved him a lot of suffering."

"But that ain't why he did it."

"Why he did it don't mean shit. The end result is still the same. The man ain't suffering no more."

I thought it over and nodded.

"What're you two bitch-weasels yapping about?" Abel said climbing on his horse.

"Nothing," I said gathering up my supplies.

I heard the clomp, clomp, clomp of Miss Connie and Doreen's horse heading down the trail.

"Saddle up, Ike." Abel pulled a bottle of whiskey out of his saddlebag.

"How many of those you got?' I asked.

Abel unscrewed the top. "I've got... let me count in my head... I'd say I've got fuck off and mind your business. That's how many."

I looped my arms through the straps of my pack. "The way I figure since I was sent out to hire your services that makes me your boss, so how much liquor you drink is my business." I can't say why, but the longer I was with Abel the less he scared me and the more he pissed me off. My Pa's gun around my shoulder, I grabbed my horse's mane and managed to crawl on top him with the help from a tree stump as a step ladder.

Abel gave my logic some consideration and then said, "Now, that's a ballsy thing to say, kiddo. And I reckon there's some logic to what you say with the exception of one thing."

"What's that?"

"I don't give a shit if you're my boss or not. How much I drink is my business. You ask me about it again, I'll beat your ass with a switch. Understood?"

"Not much to get confused about," I said urging my horse ahead of his.

"Call your bear, Ike, and let's get the hell out of here."

I heard Ike whistle as I tried to catch up with Miss Connie and Doreen.

***

At the forest break, I stopped my horse and climbed off.

"No stopping," Abel said.

I didn't acknowledge that he'd said anything. I walked until I recognized the trees where I had left my Pa's saddle and hurried to them. To my relief, it was still there under the cover I'd given it.

I heard the sound of Abel's giant feet hitting the ground. I turned to see him strip a branch off a tree.

"Boy, I said no stopping."

I picked up the saddle and carried it out of the tree line.

"Leave him alone," Miss Connie said.

"Shut up, whore! I'm tired of people mouthing off to me and disobeying my orders!"

"I ain't leaving my Pa's saddle behind."

He staggered from a belly full of drink. "You'll leave what I damn well tell you to leave behind."

"Abel," Ike said, "The boy just wants his saddle."

"You turning on me, too, brother?"

"Ain't nobody turning on you. It is what it is."

Abel thumped his fist against his chest. "I'm Abel fucking Decker!"

"You're Abel drunken Decker," Miss Connie said jumping off her horse. "We're all stopping. Nobody's eaten a damn thing all day."

"Get back on your horse!"

"Kiss my ass."

He ran towards her and without thinking, I threw my Pa's saddle in his path. Unfortunately, it had the desired effect. His foot caught on the stirrup and he tumbled to the ground, landing on his face.

I stepped back waiting for him to jump up and come after me or for my heart to jump out of my chest. It was a tossup which would come first.

He didn't move for a second or two. I begun to think I knocked him out cold or maybe even killed him.

"Abel?" Ike said leaning forward.

The bastard's shoulders shook. A quivering motion moved down his back and pretty soon his whole body started to shudder. He made a strange noise. I couldn't figure out what it was at first.

Ike looked at me and shrugged.

Abel pushed himself over on his back. He was laughing. The giant drunk bastard was laughing.

"You got salt, boy. I can see why they sent you."

"You ain't mad?"

He sat up. "Madder than hell, but that's my walking around disposition." He stood. "The lady's right. We'll eat."

We all watched him in disbelief as he walked with a limp in his gait back to his horse.

"Well, what are you waiting for? Eat I said!" He guided his horse to the foot of the hill and sat down on the ground.

Ike climb down off his horse. "I got some MREs. Army surplus in Clinton trades them out for fresh meat." He reached in his saddlebag and pulled out enough of the MRE packets for all of us. "Stew's all I got."

"Stew sounds good," I said with my eyes stuck on his brother. "Give me two. I'll take one over to Abel."

Ike tossed me two packets. "Be careful. I ain't never heard him laugh like that. Sounded almost joyful."

"Isn't that good?"

"Not when it's coming out of Abel Decker."

I wiggled out of my pack and walked over to Abel with my gun in one hand and the MREs in the other. He saw me coming and didn't grunt or growl or any of the other things I'd come to know Abel Decker to do.

"Come to shoot me or feed me?" he asked.

"Ike had some MREs."

He reached out and took one from me. "Stew. These ain't half bad, you know?"

"Never had one." I looked at him like he was about to sprout wings and take flight. I just didn't know what to make of him.

"You gonna eat or stare at me all day." He ripped his MRE open and stuck a finger in it.

I opened my MRE and scooped out some of the stew. He was right. It wasn't half bad.

"Ate my fill of these in the service. I bet I've consumed and shit out about 50,000 of these things."

"Yes, sir."

"Your Pa teach you that?"

"What?"

"That yes sir and no sir business."

"Yes, sir."

"Figured. It's a military thing."

I ate a little more and then said, "Did you really fight in the war for 32 years?"

"Lord no," Abel said with a mouthful of stew. "I served 32 tours. Each tour was about six months. You good with math?"

"Yes, sir. That's 16 years."

"That's right. Sixteen miserable years."

"That the most?"

"That's what they say. Met a fella about two years into my service that was approaching 15 years, but he got the back of his head blown off before he hit it."

"It kill him?"

Abel snorted. "Kind of difficult to walk around without the back of your head."

I laughed and then said, "Can I ask you something?"

"You can?"

"Why you being nice all of sudden?"

He smiled. "Am I being nice?"

I nodded. "Nice for you."

He shrugged. "My mind's got a tide."

"A tide?"

"Like the ocean. You seen the ocean?"

I shook my head.

"The tide is where the waves meet the land. Sometimes it comes way up on shore and sometimes it don't make it up as far. They call that high tide and low tide. When my brain's in low tide, I'm pissed off about every shitty thing. High tide comes up, I feel a little more at ease."

"So, you're in high tide right now?"

"I guess so."

"You were in low tide before?"

"Yep."

"How long you expect you'll be in high tide?"

"Never know. Not long."

"How long were you in low tide this last time?"

"I'd say about five or six years."

I stuffed some stew in my mouth. "You remember things you do in low tide?"

He stopped just before he licked his fingers. "You asking because of that one armed fella?"

"Yeah."

"Why didn't you stop me?"

I shrugged.

"Cause you knew it had to be done."

"I guess."

"That's the fuck of it, boy. Things that need to get down ain't always good and they ain't always done by good people."

"You ain't good?"

"Hell no. Farthest thing from it. Don't let my present state of tide fool ya'. I'm calmer, but I ain't better. Those things I do when I'm pissed off at the world I do when I ain't as pissed off, too."

"Cause they need to get done?"

"More or less. That's what I tell myself anyway."

The wind blew through and bent the grass this way and that. The leaves in the trees made sounds like someone was shaking a bag of nails. I couldn't believe I was at ease sitting next to Abel Decker. He hadn't done nothing but abuse and scare the piss out of me since we met.

Doreen was running across the field near the horses waving her hands over the tall grass.

"She your girl friend?"

"Shit no," I said.

He raised an eyebrow. "I expect your Pa would slap you across the face if he heard you talk like that."

"Nah, Pa don't hit. He wouldn't for cussing even if he did. He don't mind it that much."

"He don't hit? How's he keep you in line?"

I shrugged. "Don't know. I ain't got much reason to get out of line."

"No one does, but it don't stop most people."

"I suppose."

"My old man used to hit. Fucker hit hard, and I ain't talking about no slap either. I'm talking fists." He held up his hand and balled it up in a fist. "He had sharp knuckles, too. I swear he whittled them into bony points." He held the fist to my face and slowly pressed it against my cheek. "He was big as I am now, and I was as big as you are. Would you look at that? My fist covers your whole face. You think it'd hurt if I hit you right now?"

I swallowed. His tone seemed to be changing a bit. I was beginning to think his tide was getting low. "Yes, sir. I reckon it would."

He removed his fist from my face and held it out in front of him. "You're damn right it would. And it did! Sonny-bitch used to pound me day and night when I got out of line, and I got out of line a lot."

I smiled nervously.

"You know why I got out of line so much?"

"No, sir."

"Cause I liked the beatings. Loved them. Never felt more like myself than when my old man was beating me senseless."

I froze. His tone had definitely changed. I could practically hear the tide rolling back in his head.

"You want me to beat you, boy? Make you feel good. Feel like a man."

I felt my breathing pick up in pace. "No, sir. I don't want that."

His face went sour. "My beatings not good enough for ya'."

"No, sir... I mean it ain't your quality as a person that worries me. It's the beatings themselves. I ain't interested in that kind of thing."

He ducked his head and breathed in deep. "That's enough talk for now, boy. You best scoot."

"Yes, sir."

I stood.

"Boy."

"Yes, sir."

"We don't need to have no more of these sit downs, you hear?"

"Yes, sir."

"On your way."

I walked away wondering if that would be the last time I'd ever see Abel Decker in his high tide.

***

By the time I got my horse saddled, Abel was up and shouting for the rest of us to get off our asses. It was time to go. He had slipped all the way back in to low tide.

I watched as Miss Connie struggled to get Doreen on the back of their horse. It occurred to me that it probably weren't the most gentlemanly thing to do to take the saddle for myself. My ass-bone felt all bunched up from riding bareback, but that wasn't an excuse for me to lose my manners.

"Take my horse, Miss Connie," I said.

She stopped hoisting Doreen and set her down. By the time she turned all the way to me, she was crying. "Henry Arnaught, you are an angel to offer."

"It's alright, ma'am. It ain't no big deal."

"Yes it is" She wiped her eyes and then dried her hands on her pants. "But you know as well as I do that sort of thing will set his majesty off."

I watched Abel mount his own horse. "If we do it now while he ain't looking, he won't know the difference."

Ike already sat in his saddle. "The boy's right. He's been drunk most of the trip."

Miss Connie grabbed Doreen's hand and raced over to my horse. She bent down and kissed me on the cheek before I ran to her mount. It was a warm, moist kiss that popped the hairs on the back of my neck straight up.

"Hell," Ike said, "If I'd known a kiss came with the exchange, I would have traded horses back at my house."

"Lord, Ike," Miss Connie said sitting in the saddle and reaching down to help Doreen up, "it was a peck on the cheek. You can earn one of those if you get your head out of your ass and show a little chivalry like the boy." Doreen was now sitting behind her with her arms wrapped around Miss Connie's waist. She kicked the horse and galloped towards Abel.

Ike smiled and turned to me as I took my mount. "You got to show me how that chivalry works, boy."

"Move!" Abel was already halfway up the hill.

My new horse whinnied and hopped forward enough to rock me back, almost knocking me to the ground, but I gained my balance and righted myself. I caught up to Ike who was laughing at my horsemanship.

"Was it worth the kiss?"

"What are you talking about?"

"Giving up the saddle, was it worth it?"

My ass throbbed. "It's done. Just have to grin and bear it."

We stayed twenty feet back from Abel and the others.

"What about Bob?"

Ike looked over his shoulder. "He'll most likely follow us, but we won't know it. He ain't one for socializing outside of the woods."

"He won't be no trouble in Two Notch, will he?"

"What kind of trouble?"

"I mean he won't eat nobody, right?"

"From Two Notch? Hell, he's got better taste than that." He winked and rode ahead.

***

The horses lined up in a row, and we all studied the entrance to Besser Pass. The clouds raced across the sky, and a howling wind stormed out of the canyon. Abel maneuvered his horse along the dry riverbed a few yards and then turned him back toward us.

"We ain't going through the pass."

"Today?" I asked.

"Not today tomorrow or the next day."

"But, we gotta go through the pass to get to Two Notch."

"There's another way." He did a half turn and peered up at the Canyon walls.

"That'll add a two days to our trip."

"Might," he said.

"Not to side with the boy, Abel, but it's a treacherous climb," Ike said.

"Not as treacherous as coming face to face with the Ancients on their territory. They got the whole pass booby-trapped."

"Me and Doreen made it through." I said.

"But your horse didn't." Abel goaded his horse to the left of the river bed. "'Sides, you and everyone traveling with you are uninvited guests inside the canyon."

I rolled my eyes. "They were just apples, and Doreen took'em not me."

"They're more than apples. The Ancients believe that the only worthy men are men of honor. You take the apples, you ain't worthy."

"I ain't a man neither and neither is Doreen. We're just a couple of kids." I kicked my horse and galloped to the entrance of the canyon. Just before the horse crossed over into the darkness, I pulled back on its reins. A cool whirling breeze smacked me in the face. I yelled, "I'm sorry I took your goddamn apples! You left them unattended! How's a body to know they're spoken for!" I didn't get no answer. Didn't expect to. I was just yelling to clear my mind. I pulled the horse to the left to try and shame Abel. "Can't believe you're scared. Didn't think a man like you would run from a fight."

"Ain't about being scared. It's about being smart. I can make it through the canyon. You can't, and I told you last night you figure into my renegotiating."

"I can take care of myself." With that I slapped my horse on the rump and it took off like a shot into the canyon.

"Hey!" Abel said with a grumbling roar. "Get back here."

I heard the hooves of his horse chasing after me.

Leaning forward, I gave my horse another slap on the rump and another. My legs were burning from squeezing so hard. I'd rode old Runner at top speeds plenty of times, but I always had Pa's saddle underneath me.

I looked back and seen Abel coming up fast. He must've outweighed me by almost 200 pounds, but the extra weight didn't matter a bit to his stout horse. It was running like lightning.

As I turned back to face the darkness ahead, I caught the flash of a figure standing on a ledge on the canyon wall. It was a person. There weren't no doubt about it.

A thunderous pop echoed all around me. Abel had fired his gun, not at me, but at the person I'd seen. The shadows of more people ahead of me scurried about. I yanked back on the reins. The horse stumbled and skidded to a halt. I was headed back out of the canyon before Abel could catch up to me.

He turned his horse around and It wasn't long before our horses were neck and neck headed for the open sky.

Once the sun hit our faces, Abel reached over and grabbed my horse's reins. With his teeth clamped, he said, "Get off your horse."

My horse pulled up and I jumped off.

Abel was on the ground not long after. He yanked me up by the back of my collar. "Crossing me ain't a good idea, boy."

"Let him go," Miss Connie said, climbing off her horse.

"This is none of your business."

"I'm making it my business. Unhand him."

"Ike," Abel said, "handle the whore."

Ike's eyes opened wide. "I don't think that's such a good idea."

"You saying I had a bad idea?"

Ike shook his head. "I'm saying I don't want to get between the woman and her instincts. Same as I wouldn't want to get between Bob and his instincts. Makes for uncomfortable living."

Miss Connie stopped two feet from Abel and stood her ground. "I'm not going to stand by while you take a beating to the boy."

"The beating I'm about to deliver on this boy will save his life."

"And just how do you figure that?"

"My word is law. My law is for his own good. He breaks my word, he breaks my law, he gets himself killed. The beating will help him remember that the next time he decides to disobey me."

I squirmed and kicked, but it didn't do me the slightest good.

"The boy's scared out of his mind," Miss Connie said. "That's reminder enough."

Abel shook his head. "That ain't good enough for me."

Ike cleared his throat. "Hey, Abel, I ain't trying to tell you what to do, but you beat the boy like you want to, he ain't gonna be much for traveling up the canyon for awhile, and I tell you the truth, I don't think it's such a good idea to be caught down on the riverbed once night falls. We'll be easy pickings for our friends in the pass."

The expression on Abel's face eased. He loosened his grip and my feet were firmly on the ground again.

"You got a habit of letting this boy off the hook, Ike."

"Well, his troubles always seem to be chased by practical solutions, and you know me, I'm a practical man."

Abel smirked. "You ask me, I think you're fond of him, and the ladies, too. That's a shame."

Ike didn't respond.

"And what is so wrong with caring for other people?" Miss Connie asked.

"Gets you killed." He completely released me and took a step back. I had just let myself relax when I felt the weight of his palm pound into my ear. The whole side of my head went numb, and I could hear a loud ringing.

Miss Connie wrapped her arms around me and spun me around, placing herself between me and Abel. "You animal!"

"Had to give him a taste of what's in store for him if he goes against my word again. He's lucky anyway"

"Lucky?" Miss Connie said with a screech.

"I owe him two beatings and all he got was a slap."

"Two?"

"One for going into the canyon, and another for switching horses with you back there."

I rubbed my face and hid my eyes from him. I didn't want him to see the hate he'd lit up in me.

***

Treacherous wasn't nearly a harsh enough word for what we went through climbing the canyon. There was a thin winding path most of the way that barely allowed enough room for one horse at a time. The lead horses kicked up loose rocks and dirt that caused a stir from the horses in the back. I was lucky enough to be on one of those horses in the back. The fact that I didn't have no saddle made my climb as about as terrifying a thing as I've ever done.

The trail vanished in a couple of spots, and we'd have to dismount and coax the horses up steep embankments. Most the time, it took two of us to put enough tug on a horse to get him moving.

The last twenty feet of the trek was the toughest. It was the steepest embankment we come across. It was near straight up. My horse snorted and let out a throaty whinny that was as 'bout as clear a protest you'll ever hear from a horse, but with Abel's help we got him to the top.

The top of the canyon was flat and spread out as far as the eye could see. There was nothing but red dirt and rocks laid out before us. Night was waxing, and the clouds were pretty heavy. Traveling along the table top mountain didn't seem altogether smart. A drop off could sneak up on you quick, so we traveled for another 30 minutes and found a collection of boulders that Abel determined was the perfect place to set up camp.

Ike gathered brush and sticks to kindle a fire, while Doreen and Miss Connie wandered off to do their business. Abel jumped off his horse and went off in the opposite direction of them with his mount in tow. I didn't know why, and I didn't care much why neither.

I planted myself on a boulder and rubbed my sore ear.

Ike returned with a load of brush and dropped it in a pile. "Still stinging?"

"Nah, just burns a little."

"You're lucky he held back."

"You and your brother sure do see a lot a luck when it comes to him hitting me."

Ike snickered. "Guess it's all in how you look at it. You got a remember, Abel's killed more people than he's beat. And most the people he's beat, he's done it to death."

"Maybe so, but that don't make what he done right. A man ain't supposed to hit a kid."

"Abel don't see it that way." He flicked his lighter and set a small pile of brush ablaze. "You know he once told me that he come across an enemy platoon that wasn't nothing but kids. He estimated the oldest was probably fifteen. The bulk of them was your age or younger. They were the fiercest bunch of fighters he ever come across. Took out more than half of Abel's outfit."

"That ain't no excuse for what he done."

"Not meant to be. Just an explanation. Sixteen years of war molded that man into something that nobody's got any use for…" The fire started to crack and pop. "Well, that ain't exactly true. They ain't got no use for him until they need somebody dead. That kind of thing can afflict a man."

"I guess. Still don't like him."

"Neither do I, and he's my brother."

"Why do you share your land with him?"

"For one thing, it's his land mostly. He let me in on a deal he made with the previous owners. For another, he's my brother. I've known him since the day I was born. I knew him before he left for the war when he was normal, a downright nice guy. That man is worth sticking around for."

"Must've been really something if you're willing to put up with the monster he is now."

"You know you're awful judgmental for a boy hiring a killer."

"I ain't hiring him. The town is."

"Still, you was sent to make the deal with the devil. They don't send angels to do that."

"Told you, I was sent because we was the only ones that had a horse."

"Maybe," Ike said, "but I reckon they could have gone against your Pa's wishes and sent someone of their choosing if they didn't think you was up to the task. But they didn't. They sent you. Why do you think that is?"

I shrugged.

"Cause you're made up of thinly woven moral fiber. You only think killing is wrong when it's one of yours that's getting killed. You don't object as much when the circumstances is turned around."

Truth about it is I hadn't done much thinking on killing 'til that trip. I'd put a lot into dying 'cause I'd seen it a dozen times over. But killing? I just hadn't give it much play in my mind to weigh the good and bad of it.

Miss Connie and Doreen returned from their business and found a spot to sit next to the now roaring fire. The sun wasn't nothing but a sliver cutting into the dusty mountains. We sat and talked and let a general feeling of ease take us into the star-filled night. Hours must've passed before anyone asked about Abel.

"Wandered off some time ago," Ike said in answer to Miss Connie's question.

"Lord, help us," she said. "He's probably face down drunk somewhere."

"That's a fair guess," Ike said.

"Should we go look for him?" I asked hoping the answer would be no.

"Nah," Ike said. "He can take care of himself."

The conversation continued. I had moved to the ground and was leaning against the rock I had been sitting on earlier. It was about as comfortable as a person can get using a rock as a cushion. A whisper of wind blew out of the darkness and caught my attention. I looked out into the dark and it came again. It made a noise like a voice. In fact, it made a noise like several voices. The others around the fire didn't react, so I wasn't too alarmed. I sat up a little straighter and tried to get a bead on the voices, if they even were voices. I told myself on more than one occasion that it was just the wind, but I listened to myself as 'bout as good as other people listen to me, barely at all.

I was about to give up on hearing the voices again when I heard, "Go left. Not that left, the other left."

I stood up.

"Going somewhere, boy?' Ike asked.

"We got company," I said looking for my Pa's army issue. Couldn't figure on how I'd lay something like that about without knowing exactly where it was. I was a stupid kid in a lot of ways.

Ike didn't stand right away. He turned in every direction looking for the company I spoke of, but couldn't spot them. "What makes you say that?"

"I heard voices."

Ike reached in his pocket for one of his cigarettes. "It's just the wind. It'll play tricks on your ears."

"Howdy, folks," the wind said.

Ike jumped to his feet.

Miss Connie grabbed Doreen and pulled her in close.

"Who said that?" Ike asked.

A spindly man covered in dust from head to toe stepped out of the dark holding my Pa's army issue at the ready. "I did, Mr. Jolly." He smiled and I counted at least three missing teeth.

"What do you want?"

The man's smile grew bigger. "Well, now there's a long list of things I want. World peace, a fitting temple to God, a place where my children can grow up playing with my fellow man's children, and everyone gets along just skippy-fine."

Ike looked at me and shrugged. "We ain't got none of that."

The man laughed. "You ain't got none of that! That's a good one. Billy, you hear that? Man says he ain't got none of that."

A short skinny man stepped out of the darkness on the other side of the fire holding a large homemade knife. "Heard it, Cap. He's a regular comedian."

The man called Cap wiped a string of snot from his nose. "You made me snot myself, Mr. Jolly."

"My name ain't Jolly."

"Didn't think it was. I just call things like I see them. You're fat, so I see you as jolly. Works like that."

"Why not just call me fat."

"Cause that would be rude." He aimed the gun at Ike's head. "You calling me rude?"

"No, just trying to get my mind behind your reasoning."

Cap held the gun up a few seconds longer and then slowly brought it down and relaxed. "Can't fault you for that. Us being strangers and all. Maybe we should get on to the introductions. Whatcha think, Billy, should we introduce ourselves?"

"Sure thing, Cap."

"Let me guess," Ike said, "You're Cap, and he's Billy."

"Picked up on that, did ya'? But there's more."

Six more skinny, dirty people stepped forward, forming a half circle around us. In all, there were six men, a boy, and a woman in Cap's group.

Cap named them off. "You know me, and you met Billy, but from left to right over there is Jimmy, Mickey, Scotty, Scotty Junior, Pudge, and Pie."

"Pie? The woman's name is Pie?"

"Because she's sweet as, and she can whip up a nice apple pie when we got the flour."

The homely woman who was more bone than meat smiled and showed nothing but gums.

Ike smiled and turned away from her as quickly as he could. "It's nice to meet you all, but like I said we ain't got nothing you want. We can offer you a seat around the fire, but that's about it."

"Hold on now, you ain't introduced yourself. Now who's being rude?"

Ike rolled his eyes. "I'm Ike. That's Henry, Connie, and Doreen."

"And the other fella? Where's he?"

"Other fella?"

"The big fella. The one come up the mountain with ya'."

Ike hesitated before he answered. He was probably thinking the same thing I was. These people had been tracking us since we started our climb. That can't be good. "That'd be Abel my brother. Abel Decker." He said the name loudly to give it more pop. He was hoping they knew the name and the man behind the name.

"He somebody famous?"

"Infamous more like it," Ike said.

"Well, where is this infamous fella?"

"Around."

"Around ain't here."

"He's bound to show, and like I said we ain't got nothing to offer ya'."

"You got plenty of what we want." He was looking more threatening by the second.

"Not if you came looking for world peace and the like."

Cap laughed again. "I was just joshing 'bout that. I don't care nothing about world peace or children playing, blah, blah, blah. That's all from a horse shit speech I heard a fella give right before he got his head blowed off by somebody who wasn't interested in the same things."

"Oh," Ike said. I saw him start to slowly move his hand toward the inside of this coat. He was moving so slow you wouldn't know it unless you were keeping a close eye on him.

"What do you want then?" Miss Connie asked.

Cap looked at her and licked his lips. "You have got the voice of an angel, Connie. I swear I ain't never heard nothing so pretty. Billy, you hear that?"

"Heard it, Cap."

"Don't she sound like an angel?"

"Like listening to God himself talk."

"God?" Cap's tone shifted to anger. "I said an angel, not God. She can't be both. You trying to outshine me, Billy?"

Billy looked scared but not that surprised by Cap's turn. "No, sir, Cap. I misspoke. She's an angel all the way. I can see that now."

Cap took a deep breath and painted a smile on his face. "Sorry about that, angel. We shouldn't fight like that in front of y'all. Hard to conduct business like we usually do with a pretty lady like you around."

I looked at Ike and he was still moving his hand. He was staring holes through Cap.

I decided I needed to pick up the conversation to keep their minds off Ike. "That's my Pa's army issue."

Cap looked at the gun. "It is? Really?"

I nodded.

"Hell, I just found it laying over there by that pile of rocks. I didn't know nobody had a claim to it. You want it back?"

I studied his face. He looked sincere enough to mean it. "That'd be nice."

"Okay, I'll give it back after."

"After what?"

"After I shoot Mr. Jolly over there for going for that piece he's got under his coat."

Ike stopped moving his hand.

"That's better," Cap said. He moved in closer to the fire and took a seat on a rock. "Now, the lady with the voice of an angel asked a question that I aim to answer. This here's our mountain. We own everything on it and everything the passes over it. You understand?"

"You want our horses?" Ike asked.

"Don't have to want'em. We own 'em. And why is that, young Henry?"

"Cause they're on your mountain."

"Bingo, son. You're pretty smart."

"So, take the horses and we'll walk down the mountain," Ike said.

Cap shook his head. "You ain't as smart as the boy, Mr. Jolly. Henry, tell Ike here why you won't be walking down the mountain."

I swallowed before I said, "'Cause you own us?"

"That a question or a statement of fact?" Cap asked.

"Statement of fact," I said.

Ike cleared his throat. "You can't own people." Apparently he forgot he was willing to trade for Two Notch women.

"We don't think of you as people so much. More like livestock."

Miss Connie's face went sheet white. "You're cannibals?"

"We are, but we try to be friendly about it." He stood. "Now, if you folks would be so kind as to get a move on. We got a good hike back to our little village."

We didn't move fast enough for him, so he motioned with a head nod and his people descended on us. Pie yanked Miss Connie up by her hair. Scotty Junior pulled on Doreen's arm until she was on her feet. Pudge moved in on me, and I lifted my fists ready to fight. He grinned and landed a punch on my chin before I could blink. It was just hard enough to make my eyes water, but no so hard as to put me on the ground.

Jimmy, Mickey, and Scotty surrounded Ike. Two of them held his arms back, while the other robbed him of his gun.

"Easy, now," Cap said. "Remember, we're friendly cannibals."

They rounded us up and herded us into the darkness. The clouds zipped past the moon giving us brief glimpses of the terrain we were headed into. It was flat and peppered with cabbage high plants. It didn't look like there was nothing but nothing for miles.

An hour of walking, and we reached a group of rundown buildings. They were probably fairly nice structures at one time, but now they were nothing but holes separated by slots of wood. They were pitiful forms of shelter.

"Like our town?" Cap asked.

"It's a regular thriving metropolis," Ike said.

"I know you meant that as an ironic slight, but fella, this here used to be a glorious wonder for a city. Buildings, people, streets, we had the best of everything. Hope to again someday."

"What happened to it?" I asked.

"Hunger's what happened," Cap said. "Terrible, terrible hunger. Run out of food. The world cut us off, mostly because of those goddamn Ancients on the pass. People didn't have no choice but to eat one another. Had a system at first. Ate the lawbreakers. Turns out that kind of thing's quite the deterrent. People stopped breaking the law. So, the town council kept moving the laws back to the point where simple things like sneezing in public was an offense punishable by eating. Then one day, a group of us on the west side of town broke into a town council meeting and tried to reason with'em." He laughed. "They weren't too reasonable, so we killed them and butchered them right there on the spot. Divided up the meat and went back home to our families. After that it was every neighbor for themselves."

"You the last of the town?" I asked.

"Can't say for sure. Might be. We stay on our toes just in case."

"If it's food you want," Ike said. "I got a whole woods' full of meat, and there's at least three towns around here that are a day or two away."

Cap nodded. "Yeah, we know about the towns. We've been plenty of times. We steal a boy here and a girl there. Sometimes we get hold of an adult."

"Steal?"

Cap smiled. "I'm afraid we got a taste for people meat. Didn't plan on it, but God help me if it ain't the only thing that settles our hunger."

"That's sick," Miss Connie said.

"Oh, it is, Angel. It is indeed, but ain't nothing to be done about it except feed our hunger." He approached her and give her a good sniff. "Now, my plans is to take you off the menu if you don't prove to be too hard to break."

Ike stepped towards him, and caught an elbow from Scotty to the back of the head.

"Don't plan on no hero actions, Mr. Jolly," Cap said. "You make trouble and we'll take you a piece at a time and keep you alive 'til we're ready to pluck the heart from your chest."

I stepped forward with my hands raised so I wouldn't get an elbow from Pudge. "You gotta let us go, Mr. Cap. I got a town that needs our help."

He pursed his lips and studied me. "What town?"

"Two Notch."

"Two Notch? The one run by that she-demon Old Kelly?"

"Yes," I said.

"That town's beyond your help, son. You're better off being food."

"Can't hardly see that," I said. "My Pa's counting on me."

"What's your name again?"

"Henry Arnaught."

"Well, Henry Arnaught, we'll pay your daddy a visit and make sure he don't hold you in too much blame for failing. Once he finds out we ate you, he's liable to swell up with forgiveness. We'll eat him, too. Bring you two together again."

He got my goat. "You hurt my Pa, and I swear I'll kill you where you stand."

Cap laughed. "The wee one's raising up on me!"

The others joined in for a good laugh.

"Alright, let's just calm ourselves. Pie, you and Pudge run over to the kennel and fetch us stock to butcher. Get that lady with nice size rump."

Scotty sheepishly raised his hand.

"Got something on your mind there, Scotty?"

He kept his eyes down and away from Cap. "I'd just assume eat the fat one. He's bound to be tender and pack a lot of taste."

Cap looked Ike over. "You do make a good point, Scotty, but I'm going to have to say no. The way I figure he's still going to be fat next week. We can prepare a fine feast with him as the main course, but tonight I think we best dip into some of our existing stock before they give into consumption or some other sickness. Waste is the worst kind of sin in this day and age."

"You want us to take these folks to the kennel?" Pie asked.

"Now that is a fine idea, little Miss Pie," Cap said with a smile. "Leave the angel. Take the rest." He handed Pie Ike's gun.

Pudge and Pie both pushed on Ike to get him moving and they had to pull on Doreen to get her away from Miss Connie. I went without incident.

The kennel was an old inn made up of six rooms. Pudge opened a door to the first room, walked inside and let out an angry howl.

Pie guided us to the door and we looked inside. Two young boys were hanging from the ceiling, next to the lady with the nice size rump.

"They hung themselves," Pudge said cutting one of the boys from the ceiling.

The smell of rotting bodies wafted out of the room.

"Been more than a couple of day, judging by the stink," Pie said covering her mouth and nose.

"Just the little ones," Pudge said. He slapped the lady's backside. "The woman's dead no more than an hour or two."

"Least there's that," Pie said. "Meat's turned on the boys. The woman's still edible." She shook her head. "This isn't going to set with Cap."

"He's is going to be mad," Pudge said. "We was supposed to check on them yesterday. He's gonna know we didn't. He's gonna let out on us. Lord, he'll take my hand or tongue and sure as shit make me eat it!"

"He's gonna let out on you. I'm his woman. Worst he'll do is slap me around a bit."

"You ain't his woman no more," Pudge said. "He's got that pretty lady all lined up now."

"That plump bitch? Cap ain't got his sights on her."

"You heard what he said. She's off the menu."

I jumped in. "Why don't you just tell Cap the boys ran away?"

"What?" Pudge asked.

"Carry them off somewhere and tell Cap they got loose."

"He'll still be mad," Pie said.

"Not as mad," Pudge said. "He'll yell and fuss, but that's about it. It ain't a bad idea."

"It ain't a good idea, neither. The boy here will rat us out and if he don't the fat one will and if he don't, the girl will."

"None of us will," I said, "If you promise me one thing."

"What?"

"Let the girl go." I put my hand on Doreen's shoulder.

Pudge and Pie looked at each other.

Pie said, "Can't do it."

"You're Cap's woman, ain't ya'," I said.

"I am."

"Then there ain't no problem. She's skinny anyway. Small. Ain't got enough meat on her to cook."

She smiled. "He may want to keep her for breeding."

"She's barren," I said sounding more excited than I should.

"She's barren?" Pudge asked. "How do you know?"

"Her momma said. She was born with her insides twisted. She's dry."

"The boy makes a case," Ike said. "You'll avoid a solid wrath from Cap if you go his way."

"Shut up," Pie said.

"I'm in line with them," Pudge said.

"Shut up! I gotta think this through."

"C'mon, Pie, please…"

Pie struck him in the temple with the heel of her hand. "Shut the fuck up!"

We all eased off her while she ran the plan over in her mind.

"We're both dead if Cap finds out what we done," Pie said.

"He won't find out," I said.

"That's right he won't," Pudge said. "They'll keep their word. Won't you, fellas? You won't say nothing."

"Not a word," Ike said. "Let the girl go."

"C'mon now, Pie. Cap will come down on you for sure if he takes to that woman. He may be your man, but he's a man first. He'll hop on strange when he finds a shine in someone. That's just the way it is. He'll trade you out first chance he gets. You go back and tell him we let the boys go dead for a couple of days, that just might be enough to push him to her. He calls her an angel, Pie. An angel."

"Alright!" Pie screamed the word so loud I was sure the others would come running, but time passed and no one came. She thumped me in the chest with her finger. "Boy, you turn around on me and I will poke your goddamn eyes out. You hear me?"

"I ain't gonna turn around on you. Promise."

Pie sighed and run a shaky hand through her greasy hair. "Go on, girl. Get on out of here."

Doreen stepped back and scanned all our faces.

"Get on, Doreen," I said. "They done set you loose. You're able to run free. You hear me? You're ABLE to run free." I winked.

She backed away with a grin and then sped off into the night.

Pudge giggled. "Guess she don't care a piss pot about you two fellas. She run off with a smile."

"She's simple," I said.

"We gotta work up a story," Pie said. "How'd we lose three young'uns."

"Blame me," Ike said.

"How?"

"I tried to wrestle the gun from ya'. The boys and the girl broke off. Pudge came to your assistance. Y'all managed to hold onto the gun, but you lost the little ones in the struggle."

"That's good," Pudge said. "That's fucking good."

Pie agreed. "Carry the boys off, Pudge. Throw them off the west ridge."

"The west ridge? That's an hour's walk without lugging two dead boys."

"The longer you're gone the better. Make it look like you're putting in time to find the runaways."

Pudge slammed his fist into the door. "It ain't fair. I gotta do all the work."

"Yeah, well I gotta sell the story to Cap. You want to do that?"

He didn't hesitate. "Hell no."

"Get on with it then."

Ten minutes later, Pudge was headed west with one dead boy on each shoulder.

Pie had Ike cut the lady down "Drag her out front."

Ike did as told.

"Turn her face down."

Ike squatted down, put his hands underneath the dead woman's back and turned her over. Before he could stand back up, Pie fired a bullet into the back of her head.

After the shock of the gunshot lifted she said, "Figured the lady tried to escape, too."

"You could have told me you were going to shoot her," Ike said. "I nearly shit myself."

"Shut up and put her in that wheelbarrow over there."

Scotty and Mickey come running up on us. They were wheezing and gasping for a clean breath.

Mickey was the first to gather himself enough to speak. "What was the shot about?"

"Lady tried to run, so I shot her," Pie said.

Scotty looked over the body in the wheelbarrow. "She went cold fast."

"You become some kind of medical expert since I last seen you?" Pie asked.

"Me? Nah."

"Then how the fuck do you know how long it takes a body to get cold?"

"I've butchered enough to get a good idea."

"Every person's different, Scotty. Goddamn, even a pea brain like you should know that. You butcher everybody on the planet?"

"No."

"Then keep your opinions to yourself."

"Where's Pudge?" Mickey asked.

"Run after the two boys and the girl."

"You let them get away?"

"Couldn't be helped. The fat one went after the gun. Me and Pudge had a time keeping him from getting it. Everyone 'cept that one over there… Henry is it?"

I nodded.

"Everyone but Henry made a run for it."

Mickey approached Ike. "I knew you was going to be trouble," he said, landing a punch on Ike's throat.

Ike went down to his knees with his hands wrapped around his throat.

I started for him, but Scotty knocked me to the ground with little effort.

"Well," Mickey said, "I suppose we should go help Pudge round the young'uns up."

"You'll do no such thing," Pie said.

"Why not?"

"I need help lugging this big-assed lady to the butcher hut, and you're the best cutter we got, Scotty."

Scotty smiled broadly at the compliment.

"You don't need me then," Mickey said. "I'll go help Pudge."

"No, you won't," Pie said. "You'll make sure these two are secure. We've lost enough stock, so you best stand watch until someone comes to get you."

"You sure are acting bossy, Pie."

"I'm what's called the alpha bitch, asshole. Now do what I say."

The two men shared a glance and then set out to see Pie's orders through. She couldn't help but smile as she walked off with Scotty and the big rump lady they planned to butcher.

***

The stench didn't leave the room with the bodies. It was a struggle not to vomit every five minutes, but somehow we managed. Ike stretched out on the ragged mattress, and I paced about trying to clear my mind.

"You do realize we sent a mute girl to fetch my brother for help, right?"

I did realize it, but I was confident that she'd find a way to get her message across. "Doreen won't let us down."

"Can she write?"

I shrugged. "Never seen her write."

"Can she talk at all?"

"Never heard her talk? But I'm pretty sure she can if she has to."

"I ain't too confident in our plan, young Henry."

"You reckon Miss Connie's alright?"

"Well," Ike said, "she's in the company of a bunch of cannibals whose closest thing to having relations with a woman is to either eat one, or have their way with that Pie lady. I reckon things don't look too good for our Miss Connie."

"I just don't understand why Abel up and left us like that."

"That's Abel. He likes time to himself."

I plopped down on the bed. "He's peculiar as hell, your brother."

"Skilled people usually are."

A noise rose up outside the door. Someone was approaching. Me and Ike froze and tried to force the quiet into the room so we could get a clear fix on the commotion. Everything sounded muffled. Someone let out a pained groan. I stood and walked slowly to the panel covered window. I pressed my ear against it. Two voices. Men. They were whispering, but getting closer. Closer. Closer.

I near jumped out of my skin when Pudge come crashing through the door. He fell to the floor bloodied and bruised, basically beat all to hell. He brought his right hand up, and I seen two fingers were gone.

Abel stepped through the door with his gun out and a sour expression. "What the hell is wrong with you people?"

"She found you," I said.

"The mute? She found me. Fucking lot of good she was. Grunted and growled like a rabid animal."

"How'd you find us?" Ike asked.

"Found this sonny-bitch carrying two dead boys like sacks of potatoes. He give up the information I wanted."

"Bastard took my fingers," Pudge said sliding back on his elbows.

"Just two," Abel said.

"Don't matter how many. There weren't no call for it. I told you what you wanted when he drew your gun. Can't see the sense in taking my fingers."

"Took one for each boy you was carrying." He aimed the gun at Pudge's head. "How many more of you are there?"

"Seven," I said.

"Didn't ask you," Abel said putting more pressure on the trigger.

Pudge closed his eyes tight. "The boy's off by one. He ain't counting Mickey. The fella you stuck out there. We're down to six besides me. But one's just a kid."

"The leader?"

"His name's Cap. Please, don't shoot!"

"Where are the others?"

"I don't know."

"A man and woman went to the butchering hut," Ike said. "The last time we saw the others they were about a quarter of a mile East of here."

"Where's the butchering hut?" Abel asked Pudge.

"Out the door to the left. Two buildings over. Don't shoot, mister."

"I ain't gonna shoot." He eased off the trigger and put the gun in his jacket. "Sit on the bed."

Pudge did as instructed.

"Put your feet together."

"Why?"

"Don't make me pull my gun out."

Pudge put his feet together.

"Boy, get down there and wrap up his ankles in a tight hug."

I wanted to ask why, but I was afraid it would cost me two of my fingers, so I got down on the floor and wrapped my arms around his ankles.

"Hold his arms back, Ike."

"C'mon, mister," Pudge said, "I ain't argued with you or put up no kind of fight. There ain't no reason to bind me."

"You won't be bound long."

Ike grabbed Pudge's arms and pulled back.

"I can't stomach cannibals," Abel said pulling a knife from his belt. He covered Pudge's mouth with his hand. I felt blood rain down on me as he ran the knife across the cannibal's neck. The dying man gurgled and gasped for air. His body contorted and jerked. It was like I was grappling with a pig. It wasn't long before his legs just give out. There weren't a drop of life left in them. I held on tight wondering if this counted as me killing a man.

Abel walked to the door. "You can leave his legs go now, boy. He ain't going nowhere."

I got to my knees and shivered at the feeling of blood running down my back. Ike looked as ashamed as I felt. He may have seen people die in ugly ways, but I'm guessing he didn't have much of a hand in it until now. He let Pudge's arms go and the corpse balanced on the end of the bed for a short time before tumbling to the floor.

I took a seat on the bed again and looked out the door. Doreen stood just past the doorway studying the dead body with wide eyes. That's when I realized she'd seen us kill the man. It wasn't the same as seeing a man being attacked by a bear. This was people killing people. That kind of thing probably don't set too well with a skinny little mute girl.

I watched with hatred in my heart as Abel grabbed his horse's reins and took his mount. The bastard made me take part in a killing. It didn't matter a whit to me that the man we killed was planning on eating us. Abel could've killed Pudge without no help from me and probably even Ike, too. Pudge was scared dumb. He couldn't have put up much of a fight. The killer I was sent to hire seemed determined to pass along his trade to me. It wasn't a skill I cared to develop no further.

"Get off your asses!" Abel said walking his horse in a circle.

Ike stood and glanced at Pudge slumped over on the floor as he headed for the door. "What's done is done, boy. Let's get Connie and get the hell out of this town."

I couldn't move. It felt like I'd been ripped from my body, and I didn't have no control over it. I couldn't shift my eyes from Pudge until I felt something touch my hand. I worked up all the will I could to see what was touching me. Doreen had lain her hand on mine.

She smiled sweetly.

"He's dead," I said for no particular reason. She knew he was dead. I didn't need to announce it to her.

She tugged on my hand.

"Boy!" Abel said with a spiteful growl.

I stood and let Doreen pull me out the door. I seen Mickey to my right, grasping at his bloody throat and spitting up streams of blood. He was just about done.

Abel gave me a disapproving scowl. "First stop is this butcher's hut. They armed?"

"Got my gun," Ike said. "Probably got plenty of tools to cut meat with, too."

"Where's your Pa's army issue, boy?"

"That fella Cap's got it," I said.

"Well, we've gotta kill these next two as quiet as we killed this one. I'd like to hold on to the element of surprise until we get that army issue back." He bent over and held out his hand. "Come here, girl."

"What you want with her?" I asked.

"Don't worry yourself about it." Abel said. "She plays into my plan. That's all you need to know."

Doreen started toward him, but I stopped her. "I'd as soon you leave her out of your plans."

"Don't test me, boy."

I still held her back.

"She ain't gonna get hurt."

Doreen pushed my hand away and walked to Abel. He lifted her on the back of his horse before I could say another word.

"The girl will stand at the door. When they come out to investigate, I'll cut their throats. Simple as that." He quided the horse and headed for the butcher's hut. Ike and I ran behind them, but we couldn't keep up.

Abel stopped the horse in front of the hut. He motioned for Doreen to stay put. A scratch of light came through the side paneling of the house. Abel tiptoed up to it and looked inside. Satisfied with what he saw, he tiptoed back to the horse and helped Doreen down. I seen him lean over, give Doreen his instructions and then pull that horrible knife from his belt. He then nodded to Doreen and stepped back into the shadows behind the open door. Doreen stood there for several seconds before we heard Scotty.

"What the…?"

Ike pulled me to a row of dead shrubbery and yanked me to the ground.

Scotty ambled out the door. "Pudge bring you back?"

Doreen didn't acknowledge him.

Abel jumped out of the shadows, covered Scotty's mouth with his hand and cut the butchering bastard's throat. I was a good distance away, but I could've sworn I heard the blade cut through the tendons and meat.

Abel dragged the body to the side and motioned for Doreen to stay put. He stepped back in the shadows again and whistled.

We heard Pie say, "Girl, what are you doing here?" She stepped outside the door and didn't even have time to ask Doreen another question before Abel had her by the hair and was pulling her head back. He cut her throat so deep, her head near fell off.

Ike and I ran to the butcher's hut.

"That leaves us with four." Abel said going through Pie's pockets.

"Three really," I said. "One ain't but a boy younger than me."

"Good, you can kill him," Abel said. He stood. "Can't find your gun, Ike. Must be in the hut. Go get it, boy."

"Why me?"

"'Cause I've got strategy to discuss with my brother."

His reasoning didn't sit with me, but I didn't really feel like it was the time to put up a fuss. I entered the butcher's hut and zipped my head all around looking for Ike's gun. I stepped towards the back of the room and slipped, almost busting my ass. The floor was covered in a red, slick substance. To my left was a metal table with the big-rumped lady on it. Her stomach was cut open and what I assumed was her guts was snaking out of the hole and stretching down to the floor. It was all I could do not to spew the contents of my own stomach all over the place. I looked away to settle my nerves and thankfully spotted the gun on a chair in the back of the room. I ran to it and out of the room as quick as my feet could move.

I placed my hands on my knees and breathed in and out deeply. There was no way I'd ever get the awfulness of the day out of my system, not ever, not if I lived to be a hundred.

"Got my gun?" Ike asked.

I held it up, and he took it from me. "Where's Abel?"

"On his horse."

I turned and saw Abel sitting on his horse. "I thought he wanted to talk strategy with you?"

"Didn't say a word to me."

"Then why did I have to go…" It hit me. He wanted me to see the dead lady cut open. He wanted me to slip in her blood and soak in the sharp metallic smell of her insides. He wanted me to be tortured by it all. I didn't know why, but he was bound and determined to give me a lesson in the ugliness of the world.

"What's the plan now?" Ike asked.

"The plan is I backtrack a bit to get around to where this Cap and the others are," Abel said. "I'll ride in like I ain't got a clue of what's going on. Meanwhile, you three work your way in from this side. Find a place to hide until I need you."

"How will we know you need us?" Ike asked.

"I don't expect I will." His horse galloped away.

***

He didn't need us, not to handle Cap, anyway. We hid behind a rundown house within an earshot of Cap and the others. They were sitting in plastic chairs drinking from the same whiskey bottle and smoking big fat cigars. Our horses was tied to a piece of fence that was more broke than useful.

I didn't see Miss Connie at first, not until I spotted the boy sitting on the ground by a pair of bare legs. She sat up and I seen that she was stripped of all her clothes. Her nose was bleeding and mostly bent out of shape. She had a bruise around her neck and it was pretty clear she was worn to a frazzle. The boy handed her a cup, and she took it with a shaky hand.

"Fuckers had their way with her," Ike said sounding mad as hell. "Pieces of shit." He wasn't nearly as offended that they ate people as he was by what they done to Miss Connie.

Doreen stretched out to get a look, but Ike pulled her back.

"Nothing to see, darling," he said.

The figure of a giant man on a stout horse strolled up to the men so calmly it looked like a friend was coming to pay a visit, but there weren't no mistaking who it was when he spoke.

"Evening," he said.

The group of cannibals were nearly shocked speechless by the sight of him. It took them a second or two to react. When they did, they jumped out of their seats and readied themselves for a fight. All of them except Cap, that is. Cap leaned back in his chair and perched my Pa's army issue on his lap.

"Stranger," Cap said. "How's the night treating you?"

"Shitty," Abel said. "Someone ran off with my horses."

Cap smiled with the cigar poking out of his mouth. "Just your horses?"

"No, they took some other things of interest to me. My brother. That woman over there. A kid or two."

Cap removed the cigar from his mouth. "Looks like we're the fellas you're looking for."

"Looks like."

"So, you must be this Abel Decker."

"You heard of me?"

"No, but you and your brother act like I should."

"You'd be better off if you did."

"How's that?"

"Well, you would've known better than to bring us to this point."

"And what point is that?"

"The point where I had to slit the throats of four of your fuck-bucket friends on my way over here to kill you."

Cap leaned forward and his eyes turned to slits. "What did you say?"

"You heard me."

He stood. "Billy, go check on Pie and the others."

Billy turned to do as Cap instructed, but before he could take two steps, Abel pulled his gun and shot him in the head.

"Just as soon you didn't, Billy."

Billy fell to the ground.

Abel wheeled the gun around and aimed it at Cap. Cap fumbled with Pa's gun and did his best to aim it at Abel with a steady hand.

"You Cap?" Abel asked.

The head cannibal nodded.

"Stand still, Cap. You're fidgeting all about."

Cap puffed his chest out. "I ain't fidgeting."

"There. Stand like that."

"What for?"

"I got a plan."

"Plan?"

"Yeah, with you standing like that it gives me a clear shot at your collar bones. I'm going to shoot'em both, shatter them to bits. You'll drop that gun you're having a time holding anyway and then I'm going to shoot your man over there through the head. Smack-dab in the middle of the forehead."

Cap chuckled nervously.

Abel smiled and delivered on his promise. He fired three shots before any of us could blink. Cap dropped the gun and howled in pain. Jimmy was blown of his feet by the blast.

"Oh, Lord, shit fire!" Cap said wriggling on the ground. "It burns! It burns!"

We stepped out from behind the house and ran up on the scene. Doreen and Ike attended to Miss Connie.

"That's a common reaction to both gunshots and broken bones. Sets the nerves on fire," Abel said dismounting and approaching him.

Cap was crying like a baby. "Why didn't you just kill me? Oh Lord, why?"

"'Cause I got a question for ya'."

"Question?"

"There's an apple orchard somewhere on this mountain. I've been looking for it all night, but I can't get my bearings in the dark. Figured you must know."

I looked at Ike to see if he knew what Abel was talking about, but Ike was as puzzled as me.

"Fuck you!"

"That ain't only rude, but stupid," Abel said. "Makes me want to inflict more pain on your sorry cannibal ass."

"I know where it is?" Scotty Junior said.

In the commotion, I had forgotten all about him, but there he was, standing next to Ike and Doreen as they fixed up Miss Connie.

"You'll show me?" Abel asked.

"Yes, sir, if you promise not to kill me."

"You little shit," Cap said. "You'd be nothing without me. Dead and bones, you'd be. I fed you. I kept you and your daddy alive."

"You killed and ate my ma."

Cap laughed like a crazy man. "Boy, we all ate your ma. She broke her leg, and it wouldn't set right. We couldn't take care of no cripple."

"I know," Scotty Junior said, "but now you're in the same spot she was."

Abel smiled. "Boy's got a point." He pressed the barrel of the gun under Cap's chin. "Any last words?"

"Fuck…"

Abel pulled the trigger.

Standing, he turned to the boy, "Take me to the orchard."

"Don't have to," the boy said.

"Why not?"

The boy pointed to the other side of the house where we had been hiding. "It's just over there."

It was a group of a dozen or so trees. Apparently, apples didn't grow on the ground like strawberries at all.

"Ain't many apples left, though. We took some, and the Ancients come get their share, too."

"The Ancients?" I said looking at Abel.

"We'll find what we need," Abel said. He grabbed me by my arm. "You're coming with me."

We stopped at his horse, and he pulled the canvas sack Doreen and I had taken from Besser Pass out of his saddlebag. Before he headed to the orchard he gave Ike instructions. "Give her one of your cigarettes to relax her. Stay clear of my whiskey. After you clean her wounds, get to her female area. Cannibals are disease-ridden dogs. She'll need a scrubbing inside and out."

We started toward the orchard and Scotty Junior began to follow. Abel stopped. "You stay here, boy."

Scotty Junior shrugged and sauntered back over to the plastic chairs.

We continued toward the orchard. "Can't abide fucking cannibals," Abel said.

I turned and looked at the boy sitting on a chair. "You're going to kill him, aren't you?"

Abel shook his head. "Can't. I told him I wouldn't."

I sighed. At least he was a man of his word.

"You're going to do it."

I stopped, but Abel kept walking. "I ain't neither."

"You will."

"No, I ain't."

He stopped and turned to me. "This is how it's done, boy. He's a cannibal. There ain't no cure for cannibals."

"But he's just a kid. Younger than me. Younger than Doreen."

"Age ain't got nothing to do with it. The little fucker ate his own mother."

"He didn't have no choice."

"I've been in a lot of desperate situations boy, but none have drove me to eat a relation. He had a choice."

"I don't care. I ain't going to do it."

"You do it, or I'm gone."

"Gone?"

"Back home. The marauders can have Two Notch."

I felt my blood rushing through my veins. "That ain't fair. The two things ain't got nothing to do with one another."

"They got everything to do with one another."

I stomped the ground. "Why are you so set on me killing?"

He approached me with a bitter glare. "Because you need to know the grit of it. You need to gnash your teeth into it. You need to have the stones to turn to it without a thought."

"What? Why?"

"So the next time a band a fucking marauders comes to Two Notch, your rector won't have to send a boy to find a killer to do their fighting. The boy can do the killing for them."

He didn't wait for me to respond. In fact, he was in the orchard before I even thought about moving. Eventually he called out for me to join him. For some reason, I did. I regretted the man's company more and more all the time, but he'd saved my ass, so I couldn't very well deny his requests.

He handed me the canvas sack. "Fill it up."

"Why?"

"Cause I said to."

I took the sack. "We got plenty of supplies, and to tell you the truth, I've lost my taste for apples since this whole Ancients business."

He plucked three from a branch beyond my reach. "These apples ain't for us."

"Who they for?"

"The Ancients."

I held a tiny apple in my hand. "I don't understand. Why we picking apples for people that are bent on killing me?"

"'Cause I heard a story from a traveling physician years ago 'bout a friend of his who got tangled up in the same mess as you. Stole the Ancients apples going through Besser Pass, and they stalked him for days. For whatever reason, one of the Ancients took pity on this man and left him a note that read 'Replace' They also drew him a map to a place called Cannibals' Orchard. He knew what they wanted. Replace the apples he took with the apples from Cannibals' Orchard and all would be forgiven."

"I didn't get no note."

"That's true, and I don't know if it'll get you out of their sights, but I figured it was worth a try."

I stuffed a couple of apples in the sack and counted how many we had picked. We had eight nice sized apples and a couple of runts. A thought came to me as I saw Abel stretch out for the plumpest apple yet. "You weren't afraid to go through the canyon."

"I've dealt with worse."

"This was all set up by you."

He reached the apple and picked it.

"You come up here knowing Cap and his crew would see us. You left us to get caught by them. Doreen found you so quick because you'd followed us here."

"What if I did?"

"You could have got us killed is what if."

"I had a bead on you the whole time. Wasn't nothing going to happen to you. Nothing serious anyway."

I saw Ike help a trembling Miss Connie to her feet. "What about that." I pointed in their direction.

He gave them a quick glance and returned to picking apples. "That wasn't planned."

"Not planned?"

"They went at her quicker than I anticipated. Figured they wouldn't get to climbing on her at least until morning. Word is cannibals got problems with limp peckers. Guess that word is false."

I was spitting mad. I wasn't even sure what exactly it was they had done to her. All I knew was that she was hurt bad. My eyes landed on a rotten apple lying on the ground, and I picked it up and heaved it at Abel. It splattered against his lower back.

"Damn it!" He said wiping the gook from his back.

"You had no right to use us as bait! No right! Miss Connie is hurting."

"Boy, I did it for you!"

"What?"

"Shit, you're dense. I didn't need to find this orchard for me. The Ancients ain't on my tail. They ain't hunting me down."

I felt a pressure on my shoulders like I was holding up the whole world. "Me?"

"I stink like turned apple thanks to you."

I stood stunned and processed the events of the night in my muddled brain. This was all about me. Miss Connie was in the condition she was in because of me. "Why would you do it? You don't even like me?"

"It ain't got nothing to do with whether I like you or not. Tired of being bothered by the stalking. If this can give me a minute's rest, we're going to do it..." He stopped mid sentence and looked past me.

I turned to see Scotty Junior standing next to an apple tree holding my Pa's army issue aimed at Abel.

"Boy like you ought not play with a gun like that." Abel said.

Scotty Junior glared at him. "Ain't playing."

"You best lower it, boy."

"Can't shoot ya' if'n I ain't aiming it at ya'."

"You ain't got no call to shoot me, boy. I agreed to spare you."

"You didn't spare my Pa. Slit his throat. You said it yourself." The weight of the gun was working against him. It would drop, and he'd muscle it back up.

"Your Pa was one of them, huh?"

"He was."

"Well, guess that means you'll be eating him, then."

The boy shrugged. "Got plenty of meat to choose from thanks to you."

"Look, Scotty Junior," I said, "Don't kill him."

"Why?"

"'Cause I need him."

"Don't interest me none what you need." He pulled the red trigger and cried out when the butt of the gun popped him in the chin on the recoil. I could hear his teeth breaking from the blow. He stumbled back into an apple tree and dropped the gun. I darted for it, and scooped it up before he could recover.

I turned my attention to Abel. He was sitting flat-assed on the ground. He wasn't moaning or showing any indications of being shot. I run over to him and saw he was holding his stomach with his left hand. "You shot?"

"I'm shot." He stuck out his cupped hand and showed me a little pool of deep red blood.

"Is it bad?"

"It ain't good," he said with a chuckle. "Told you cannibals were for shit."

I stood with fire in my eyes. Abel Decker was a bastard, but he was my bastard. I felt all kinds of mad taking over my body. I checked the gun to make sure it was loaded even though I knew it was and stormed over to Scotty Junior who just getting back his senses. Out of the corner of my eye, I saw Ike, Miss Connie, and Doreen approaching. They were there, but they might as well not have been. I felt like it was just me and the little jack-ass cannibal left on the planet. I raised the gun.

"He killed my Pa," Scotty Junior said raising his hands.

"I told you I need him."

"Don't kill me. Please." He was crying and that made me even madder.

"Henry, don't!" I heard Miss Connie say.

A trickle of doubt crept into my brain.

"Please!" Scotty put his hands together, begging for his life.

"You're a cannibal, boy. There ain't no hope for you." I pulled the trigger.

***

We were in one of the cannibal's houses before I could even hold a thought. I hadn't a clue what happened from the time I shot Scotty Junior to the time I found myself sitting on the rotting wooden staircase of a decrepit old house. I heard voices and followed them with a slow head turn to my right. Miss Connie was tending to Abel's wound with Doreen's help.

Ike walked into the house from the porch. "They ain't got shit for bandages or medical supplies in this town, if you can even call it that," he said to Miss Connie.

"I'll work with what I got," she said.

Ike noticed that I was listening to their conversation. "Look who decided to join us."

"He going to make it?" I asked.

"Hard to say. Gut shots generally don't turn out well, but then again, we ain't talking about any old gut there are we? That's Abel Decker's gut."

"He looked like he was bleeding out in the orchard."

"That man don't need blood to live. All he needs is whiskey and mean."

I was struck by a wave of panic. "Where's my Pa's gun?"

"Relax," Ike said, "It's right there." He pointed to a corner wall near the front door.

I jumped up and rushed over to it. Holding it, I saw myself pulling the trigger in the apple orchard. "Scotty Junior?"

"Dead. That kind of thing is bound to happen to you when you got a hole the size of a fist in your chest."

"Abel should have shot him after he told us where the orchard was. We wouldn't be in this mess."

"He gave the boy his word…"

"Look where his word got us."

"Calm down, Henry. Miss Connie will get Abel going again. He's tougher than dried leather. We'll get to Two Notch."

I nodded and stepped out on the porch. I wasn't thinking about Two Notch. I was thinking about me. If Abel had just killed Scotty Junior when he had the chance, I wouldn't have had to. And it wasn't just that I had to kill him that bothered me so much. I wanted to kill him. I wanted the little cannibal shit dead for what he did to Abel. I didn't like that kind of want creeping around in my head.

I looked back in the house and watched Miss Connie take care of Abel. She turned my way and gave me a head nod. I could tell by her eyes that she didn't see me the same way anymore. She seen me pull the trigger on a boy begging for his life. It didn't matter to her what he was. She had this idea he didn't deserve to die. Maybe she didn't have same idea about me anymore.

Just before sunrise someone poked me awake. I opened and fluttered my eyes into focus and seen Abel hovering over me. He was pale and gray. His eyelids drooped, and he was drenched in sweat. "Up, Henry." He was breathing heavily through his nose, and it caused him to release a whistling sound with each breath he took in.

I got up to my knees too fast and took to feeling myself spin. Placing one foot on the sagging hardwood floor, I worked to right myself. I had drifted into a deep, deep sleep and couldn't remember how I got there. I barely remembered lying down on the floor. "You, okay?"

"No," he said taking slow small steps with his arm pressed against his belly.

I stood and saw Doreen near the door rubbing the sleep out of her eyes. Miss Connie and Ike were sound asleep on the other side of the room. "What are we doing?"

"Leaving."

"Now?"

"Yes, now."

Doreen bent down and picked up the sack of apples.

"You don't look like you're in no condition to ride."

"I can ride. You and the girl are going to do the hard part anyway."

Doreen walked out of the house slumped shouldered carrying the apples.

I stopped. "What are you talking about?"

Abel propped himself up on a dusty, weathered chair. "You gotta undo this apple thing, you and the girl. Can't anybody else be involved."

I stiffened. "You want us to go through Besser Pass?"

"Not exactly. "There's a cave…"

"No," I said. "We ain't got time for that. If you can ride, we got a get to Two Notch. Time is running out."

"Don't argue with me on this, Henry." He leave go of the chair and headed out the front door.

I followed. "They're just apples, Abel. Me and Doreen is sorry we took'em, but we can deal with that business after we save Two Notch."

"Gotta deal with it now."

"I don't see why…"

"Henry!" He stopped on the front property of the house, and I could see him sway. "You can't put things like this off. Don't let the ghosts run you down, son. Believe me I know what I'm talking about."

"I don't see how because you ain't making no sense."

He continued toward the horses. "The things you do in this world will catch up to you. That's all you gotta know. You don't deal with them when you got a chance they will deal with you. This is your chance."

"But they're just apples."

He turned and his gray face streaked red, "They ain't just apples! Not to the Ancients! I done told you that! They are a measure of a traveler's worth. The Ancients hid themselves away because they saw the world turn sour. People took and they took and they took until there wasn't nothing left to take." He stumbled.

I ran up to him and did my best to help him stay on his feet.

"Henry, the Ancients may be Bible thumping idiots, but they're right about one thing. The world don't need no more takers. You understand?"

"No, sir." I said helping him to the horses. Doreen was already standing next to the mare, scratching it under the chin.

"What's not clear to you?"

"I took that boy's life last night. How do I give that back?"

Abel chuckled and coughed. "You're a smart little fucker, Henry, aren't you? I can't reconcile that for you, son. I've killed more men, women, and children than I can remember. Most deserved it. Some didn't. The ugly truth of it is that it gets easier each time you do it. The first man I killed had me all turned around. I kept thinking how much God must hate me for doing such a thing. The last man I killed... that Cap fella, you know what I was thinking?"

"No, sir."

"I was thinking how much I hate God for making a man that deserved to be killed."

I knew right away who he meant. "You ain't talking about Cap, are you?"

"No, I ain't."

"Don't know what I'm supposed to do with that, sir."

"What do you mean?"

"What kind of lesson am I supposed to get out of that?"

He smiled. "Not everything's a lesson, son."

We reached his horse and I helped him get his foot in the stirrup. He grunted and pulled himself up on his mount.

I helped Doreen on the horse she and Miss Connie had been riding, and then climbed up myself. I looked at

Abel and was surprised to see a broad smile on his face. "You must be in one of your high tides."

"Henry, all my tides have run out. Gut shot will do that to you. I'm just me now."

"Why you calling me Henry all of sudden?"

"That's your name, ain't it?"

"It is, but you've been calling me boy since we met."

"Maybe it's because you ain't a boy no more." He made a clicking sound with his tongue and moved his horse toward the West.

I couldn't help but swell up with pride by his statement. "What about Miss Connie and Ike?"

"Left them a note with directions."

"Why not just wake them and have them come with us to the caves?"

"'Cause Miss Connie would throw a fit, and I ain't exactly in the condition to put up much of a fight."

Full of myself I said, "I can handle her."

He laughed. "Don't get ahead of yourself, son. Miss Connie may have looked fragile after what she went through last night, but I can promise you one thing. She's a woman that can just about out do any man in a game of wits. Me included. Do yourself a favor and find a way to stay on her good side. You'll be a lot happier for it. Trust me." He twitched and groaned, clutching his belly.

I seen blood seep through his fingers. "Maybe you ought not go with us. Me and Doreen can find it if you give us the directions."

He shook his head. "I'm escorting you there. But I do think I'll cut back on the chatter, if you don't mind."

"No, sir, we don't mind."

***

Two hours of silence later, the horses came to a stop in front of a big hole in the ground. Normally, we could have taken the trip in half the time, but it pained Abel if the horses picked up past a lumbering walk. His breathing had turned into a wheeze along the way, and the way he was slumped over in his saddle, I wasn't sure if he was even conscious.

"This is it," Abel said.

I snickered. "This ain't a cave. It's a hole."

"That's what a cave is," he said. "This one's entrance just happens to be on the ground instead of on the side of a mountain. You'll find footholds down until you hit a level surface."

"Then what?"

"Walk straight ahead."

"For how long?"

"Until they find you."

I swallowed my next breath and choked. "Find me? You mean the Ancients are in there."

"They are."

"I thought I was just supposed to leave the apples were I got 'em."

"No, ain't good enough. They're going to want to look into your eyes. See if you're doing this just to get off their list or if you're truly repentant."

"Then we're in all kinds of trouble because I'm pretty sure I'm doing this to get off their list."

He coughed and spit up a gob of red snot. "I suggest you have a change of attitude before they find you then."

I turned to Doreen and, like most times, she didn't appear to give two shits about any of it. "Let's go then," I said.

We both dismounted and I tied the end of the canvas sack shut, and then stuffed it inside my coat. We approached the hole and I began to climb down first.

"Good luck," Abel said.

He was shivering now. I could hear his teeth chattering as I disappeared down the hole. Doreen climbed down after me, and I was impressed with her climbing skills once again. She looked to be half squirrel.

We reached the bottom, and I planted myself firmly on the ground before offering to help Doreen down. She slapped my hand away and jumped down the last four feet. She hit the ground with a thud, but sprang up on her toes like a cat.

The light poured in from the top of the hole, but it didn't make it very far down the tunnel in front of us. Seemed like a stupid thing to do, walking through a pitch black cave without a light, but we didn't have a choice. I grabbed hold of Doreen's hand, and we stepped slowly through the cave.

"I hope this ain't just a fool's errand sent down on us by a dying man, Doreen."

My free hand was in front of me as I felt my way forward. I hit my head on an unseen rock on more than one occasion. The cave was filled with the sound of gurgles from water running down the walls. It increased my jitters. I ran my hand across the slimy rock and reached a corner that I could grab onto and pulled myself forward. I stuck my head past the jagged edge I had a hold of and felt a breeze run past my face. The cave opened up into a big chamber.

I yelled, "Hello!"

There was no response 'cept my echo.

"I ain't keen on going much farther," I said. "But I guess…"

A pair of green eyes appeared on the other side of the chamber. And then another. And another. I squeezed Doreen's hand tighter.

"Hello," I said.

The eyes flashed in and out as the Ancients looked at each other. One of them hissed.

"Listen, we took your apples before, and we just wanted you to know we're sorry."

The three Ancients started for us. They weren't having any trouble navigating in the dark.

"We didn't mean nothing by it. We didn't know they belonged to people… you are people, ain't you?"

They were as mute as Doreen.

"Anyway, we come to set things right." I unbuttoned my coat and pulled out the sack of apples. "We found more apples and picked some. They come from that cannibal's orchard." I held out the sack. "Can you see this?"

They weren't no more than ten feet away when they stopped moving. I couldn't see nothing but their eyes. The closer I looked them over, the more I come to realize they weren't eyes at all. They were goggles of some kind that lit up green.

"We done wrong. We took something that didn't belong to us, and that weren't our right. The girl can't talk otherwise she'd tell you the same thing."

A flash of light appeared next to the three Ancients. One of them was lighting up a torch. Once it got going, the fella or gal (I couldn't tell one way or the other) held it up, and I seen their faces for the first time. They were all bleach white and bald dressed in brown robes. Their faces was sunken and chiseled. I could pert near count the bones in their faces.

The Ancient in the middle stepped forward and took the sack from me. He untied it and sniffed the contents.

"The fella who brought us here, Abel Decker, he says y'all had to get a look at me to see if I was truly sorry for what I done, and to be truthful, I don't know if I am or not."

They craned their necks back and forth studying me.

"I mean I know it ain't right to take something that ain't yours. My Pa taught me that. But I ain't never seen apples like those before. Doreen neither... least I don't think she has. And we was hungry to boot. I know that ain't no excuse."

I heard a sound like a whisper come out of their mouths, but I couldn't make out any words.

"I know you are Godly people. I learnt that much about you, and you got it in your heads that folks who take your apples are Satan. But, I'm sorry to say I've done things since that weigh heavier on me than taking your apples. And since you're people who claim to know about God and such, I'm wondering if you can answer something for me?"

They stopped their whispering.

"I can't remember a time when I ain't had nothing except a choice between what's bad and what's worse. I mean take your apples for instance. I had a choice between being hungry or taking something that don't belong to me. And the boy I killed... I had a choice between letting a cannibal live and most likely prey on other people or kill him and make sure he wasn't allowed to go on with his cannibal ways. And then there was another cannibal I helped kill. You can see what I've been up against. So, my question is how come God ain't giving me nothing but bad to choose from?"

They looked at each other. The fella... or gal in the middle stepped forward. "God does not give you choices." The voice was so horse and gravelly that I was pretty sure it had to be a man. "God gives you wisdom."

I mulled over his statement. "I ain't sure I understand."

He smiled. "It's the best I got, kid." With that he rejoined the others. "You're forgiven." The cave went dark again and we heard, "The girl, too."

***

Climbing out of the hole behind Doreen, I seen Abel laying on the ground propped up on a rock. His eyes was half closed and he was soaked with sweat. I ran to him and knelt down.

"Abel?"

He tilted his head up. "You find'em?"

"Yes, sir."

"And?"

"It worked. You were right."

He closed his eyes and swallowed loudly. "That's a load off."

"Yes, sir."

"It's cold as hell on this fucking mountain."

I nodded, but I didn't agree. The wind blew in a small chill, but the rising sun was bringing on some heat. "What can I do for you, Abel?"

"Nothing." He grinned. "Kind of funny if you think about it. I fought in that damn war for sixteen years and came out of it with nothing but some broke bones and a couple of bullets in my shoulder. Run wild and mean when I got back. Now, I'm done in by a knee-high cannibal."

I heard the sound of horses approaching.

"You damn fool!" Miss Connie said as she galloped up on her horse bareback. She hopped off the horse before it came to a full stop.

"What the hell are you doing, Abel?" Ike asked as he pulled back on his reins. "Running off like that? You ain't had near enough time to mend."

Miss Connie knelt down on the other side of him. She touched his forehead. "You're burning up."

"The shit I am," Abel said shivering.

"You got the chills from your fever," Miss Connie said pulling back his shirt to expose his wound. It was a bloody mess. "You busted your stitches."

"Should have stitched me up better."

"We're going to have to cauterize it," Miss Connie said.

"The hell you will," Abel said through chattering teeth.

"I've got to stop this bleeding, Abel. The wound's too bad for stitches. It's the only way."

"What's cauterize mean?" I asked.

"It means your Miss Connie is a torturous bitch, that's what it means," Abel said.

"Go on and talk," Miss Connie said. "All you're going to do is make me enjoy this even more." She looked at me. "Bring me one of those spare magazines from your daddy's gun."

I hopped up and nearly tripped over Doreen on my way to my horse. I rifled through my backpack like I didn't have a second to spare, and, far as I knew, I didn't. I felt the cold metal structure of the magazine and yanked it out of my pack.

When I knelt back down beside Abel, Miss Connie was cleaning his wound with a handkerchief she must have had in her pocket. Ike was pacing by Abel's feet and Doreen was sitting on the ground next to Miss Connie watching her every move. I held out the magazine.

"Pull out a shell," she said.

I did as asked.

"Open it."

"Open it? How?"

"I don't know," she said sounding impatient. "Find a way. I need the gunpowder."

Ike ripped the shell out of my hand. "Here," he said pulling a small pair of pliers from his pocket. "For my roaches."

"You got roaches?" I asked.

He shook his head. "Never mind." He worked and grunted and gritted his teeth as he tried with all his might to pull the shell apart. Finally, after I thought his head would explode from all the effort he was giving, the tip of the shell wiggled loose from its purchase. He handed the part of the shell that contained the gunpowder to Miss Connie.

She gave me the bloody handkerchief and took the shell. "Lighter," she said to Ike.

He had it in her hand before the 'r' rolled off her tongue.

"You want something to bite on?" she asked Abel.

"Your throat," he said with a hiss.

Doreen picked up a stick in front of her and held it up.

"Perfect, honey."

Doreen jumped up and stepped around Miss Connie to get to Abel's head. He looked at her, winked, and opened his mouth. Doreen responded with a giggle and put the stick in his mouth.

"We going to have to hold you down, Abel?"

He shook his head.

"Good," she said pouring the gunpowder on and around the wound. "Huddle in close," she said to me and Ike. "Block the wind."

Abel took deep breaths in and out of his nose.

I heard the flick of the lighter and then jumped at the sight of a bright burning flame coming from Abel's belly. He bellowed through the stick.

"That's cauterize," Miss Connie said.

***

"He's done." It was hard to tell who Ike was talking to. He was standing near the horses fiddling with his hat. Had been for a time. I expect he was just saying it because no one else would.

"He's ain't dead," I said.

"He will be soon enough."

"You don't know that. Ask Miss Connie. She ain't give up on him."

Miss Connie was sitting cross-legged next to Abel. His eyes were shut and his chest was growing and shrinking as his lungs sucked in and spit out air.

"Tell him the truth, Connie," Ike said.

Her eyes begun to shine as the sadness built up in her and she rocked back and forth. "When those men, those cannibals were.... clawing at me – rubbing their filthy hands all over me. Getting their putrid stink all over me. I actually prayed. Me." She grinned. "You know what I prayed for?"

The question just hung in the air until I got the courage to say something. "To be saved?"

She laughed and blew snot out of her nose.

Me and Ike shared a perplexed glance.

She lifted her hand and wiped the snot away. The laugh turned into a cry. "I prayed that Abel Decker would come and kill every one of those fuckers!"

Doreen wrapped her arms around Miss Connie's neck and spoke in a whisper. "It's okay to cry."

The noise of the day melted away. I couldn't move. Her voice was so small and sweet. Miss Connie hugged her tight and bawled her tired eyes out. She talked. Doreen talked. It was the only time in my life that I ever heard her speak a word, and I think she done it just to let Miss Connie know that she wasn't alone.

"Holy shit," Ike said.

"Y'all are a happy bunch," Abel said with his eyes still closed.

Miss Connie released Doreen and bent over Abel. "How's the pain?"

"Painful."

"Want one of my smokes?" Ike said hurrying to his brother's side.

"And end up like you? No thanks."

I had to stop myself from dancing for joy. "I told you he wasn't dead! I told you!"

"I'm dead, "Abel said. "My body just ain't caught on yet."

"What do you want us to do?" Ike asked.

"Leave me. Go on and get to Two Notch."

"What for?"

"My current condition ain't changed Two Notch's troubles. They sent the boy to hire someone to save their flea-bitten town. Go save it. Place is crawling with Harding and his men by now."

"They sent the boy to hire Abel Decker. I ain't Abel Decker. I'm Ike Decker. Ike. The half-wit, pot smoking, waste of a man. I don't save towns. I ruin 'em…"

"Shut up with that shit, Ike." Abel opened his eyes. "You know the best part of being Abel Decker? The name wins the day ninety percent of the time. I've done bad things in my life. Things that scare the living shit out of most men. Those bad things prevented me from doing even worse things because people walk away when they hear the name Abel Decker."

"My name ain't Abel Decker," Ike said.

"Only 'cause you say it ain't."

Ike twisted his head around to get a good look at our faces. "What in the hell does that mean?"

"I think he wants you to pretend to be him," I said to Ike.

Ike scrunched his eyes.

"That smoke has burned your brain out, Ike. I couldn't say it any plainer."

"You're crazy, Abel. I can't go into Two Notch and tell them I'm you."

"Why the hell not?"

"Well, I don't look a thing like you to begin with."

"No one's seen me in close to ten years. Most everyone who knew me before that is dead. And I ain't stepped inside Two Notch but once in my life, and that was by accident. Couldn't get out of there fast enough." He coughed and spit up blood. Miss Connie quickly wiped it away.

"How about the fact I'm almost twenty years younger than you."

"Abel Decker ain't human," he said with a rasp. "Abel Decker's a fucked-up legend. Legends don't get older."

Ike crossed his arms in front of him. "This is just the dumbest thing I've ever heard. They ain't never going to buy it."

"It ain't the worst idea," I said.

"What?"

"I mean he's right. Two Notch is still in trouble."

"Listen to Henry, Ike. He'll help you sell it," Abel said.

"But I can't go up against a band of marauders."

"Fucking marauders," I said.

"Even worse."

"They ain't no match for Abel Decker," Abel said.

"How do you know?"

"I know their work."

"What work?"

"That one-armed fella."

"What about him?"

"I would've took both his arms." He grunted a lone chuckle.

"Christ almighty…." Ike kicked the dirt. "And what about the cannibals? They never heard of the great Abel Decker. What if Harding and his boys ain't either?"

"Cannibals ain't exactly in the loop on most things. They keep to themselves. How many folks you come across that don't know my name?"

Ike didn't answer right away. "None 'sides them." He placed his hands on his hips. "Damn it, Connie, you gonna weigh in on this?"

"I'll do it," she said.

"You'll do what?"

"I'll be Abel Decker."

He shook his head. "What are you talking about?"

"I'm talking about taking out a band of heartless, worthless dick slingers. You don't want to be Abel Decker then I'll do it."

"You all have lost your minds," Ike said kicking up even more dirt.

Abel smiled. "The woman's right. She should do it…"

"Shut up!" Ike dropped his chin to his chest. "I'll do it. I'll be Abel Decker and get my fat ass shot all to hell. But so help me, if you live, Abel and by some miracle I do too, I'm given you a handful of gold out of the pay and that's it."

"Gold's yours. Never wanted it in the first place."

"What the hell does that mean?"

"I was just doing this because I was bored. I was meant to do the bad that needs to get done, Ike. You know that as well as I do."

"Just 'cause you're meant to do a thing doesn't mean you have to."

"That don't make any sense at all."

"Makes plenty of sense, you fool…"

"Shut up and listen. My dog tags are in my saddlebag. Wear 'em. Far as everyone knows, I'm still a gung ho grunt. The tags will give them enough cause to believe you. Harding will probably have a man or two on watch at every point of entry to the town. Ride up slow on 'em at night." He winced in pain.

"Then what?"

Abel held his gut and blew air out of his nose. "Fucking bullet feels like it's snaking through my belly." He huffed and slowly relaxed. "Shoot the first one who speaks."

"Shoot 'em?"

"No one expects a slow rider to shoot. You shoot a man for no reason that'll convince Harding you're me."

"Won't the other man fire on me?"

"No… most likely not. He'll be too scared and confused. Marauders always put the low men on guard duty at night. The men with respect and seniority stay in town to drink and carouse. The other one will run. Let him. Better he tells Harding you shot one of his men cold than you."

"I don't like that 'most likely' business."

"Harding will puff up for his men, but if you get him alone, he'll be agreeable to your terms of surrender."

"Which is what?"

"Leave town. "

"That's it?"

"Not if it was really me, but since it's you, you best not push your luck."

"And the gold? The rector ain't agreed to that."

"She will… Henry will make sure of it. Won't you?"

"Yes, sir," I said. "She'll pay it."

"Anything else?" Ike asked.

"Yeah, smoke one of your cigarettes before you reach Two Notch."

"Thought you hated those things."

"I do, but they relax ya'. Better you're stoned than nervous. Just don't smoke enough that you can't shoot straight."

Ike fidgeted with the cuff of his jacket a few times and then said, "S'pose that's it then."

"That's it," Abel said.

Ike cleared his throat a few times. "Don't die while I'm gone, brother."

"You either."

Miss Connie stood and hugged Ike. "I'll do what I can for him."

Ike pulled her in tight and I heard him whisper, "I'm sorry for what those men did to you."

She went flush red and buried her face into his shoulder.

I felt a tap on my shoulder and turned to an awkward embrace from Doreen. It threw me, and I stumbled back a step or two before I got my footing. She quickly released me and ran back to her spot next to Abel.

After a hug from Miss Connie, Abel motioned for me to come closer.

I did as he asked.

"Ike will lose his nerve a hundred times before you reach Two Notch."

"Yes, sir."

"Your job is to help him get it back every time."

"Yes, sir."

"Remind him of the instructions I gave him."

"Yes, sir."

"If he goes down..."

"He won't.

"If he does, you ride out of there. Leave Two Notch."

"Sir?"

"Leave it, son. Don't let Harding get hold of you. You don't want no part of what he's got."

"But my Pa..."

"He'd tell you the same thing. Now say it." He grabbed hold of my sleeve.

"I'll leave it," I said.

"Good." He let go of my coat. "Meanwhile, I'll work on..." he coughed and sputtered. "I'll work on recovering. Join up with you and my brother."

I looked at Miss Connie. She shook her head.

"Let's go, boy," Ike said from his mount.

"Name's Henry," I said. "Not boy."

"Fair enough," he said. "Get on your damn horse, Henry. We've got your shithole town to save."

We reached the bottom of the mountain near the other side of the pass and climbed off our horses. Abel was right. As we rode, Ike lost his nerve about as often as he blinked . There weren't no question about it, he wasn't nothing like his brother. I worked like hell to get him back on the trail a half dozen times along the way. Did it by getting his mind off what we were riding into.

As we give our asses a break from riding I asked him, "If somebody said to you 'God don't give you choices, God gives you wisdom,' what do you reckon they meant by that?"

"Means somebody's full of shit is what it means."

"No, seriously, what I am I supposed to get from that?"

"I don't know. Why the hell you asking me?"

"Cause there ain't nobody else to ask, and you're older. You're supposed to know more than me."

"Just 'cause I know more, don't mean I know enough."

"You ain't no help."

"You give too much thought to God and such, Henry. You're way too young for those matters."

"It weighs on me."

"Steer your mind to other thoughts like girls and things."

"Girls don't confuse me."

He laughed. "They will."

"It just don't make no sense to me. God don't give you choices. God gives you wisdom."

"Lord, you just won't tear loose from it... okay, what it means is this ... and keep in mind, I don't believe none of this bullshit, but you asked. It means that God don't make shit happen. He just give you the brains to know what to do when shit happens."

"Oh."

"And as far as belief in God and the like goes, it's about the most sensible thing I've heard. That come from your rector?"

"No. In fact, she says 'bout the most opposite thing you could say about God. Says he's spiteful and angry. Always punishing us for the most minor things."

"Your rector's an ass. She don't know no more about God than me and you."

"He talks to her. Gives her visions."

"Hell, if you ask me, he didn't even give her the brains he give everybody else."

"Then how did she know the fucking marauders were coming?"

"She got word somehow. Visitor coming through. Something like that."

"We don't get many visitors. Traders every now and then is all. They don't even come 'round much no more. Nobody in Two Notch has got much to trade."

"You ask me, we shouldn't be saving Two Notch. We should be putting it out of its misery. You and your Pa should have up and left years ago."

"Pa says the dirt's got yield."

Ike smirked. "I know you love your Pa, but if he thinks the dirt out this way has got yield his brain ain't got no yield."

I shrugged and peered out towards Two Notch. It was too dark and too far away to see. But in my imagination, I could picture it, the rundown old buildings, the rundown people, the dirt and grime of it. It was ugly. It was a speck of nothing special. It was home.

Ike stretched his back and cast his eyes down on the dried riverbed coming out of the canyon. His face went sour. "Lord, help us."

"What's wrong?" I asked trying to see what held his interest in the dirt.

"Tracks. Horses," he said pointing at the marks in the dirt. "Two days old, I'd guess." His eyes bounced from track to track to track. "Shit."

"What?"

"I count a dozen horses, maybe as many as fifteen. And…" he said as he walked over and picked something off the ground and held it up. "At least one of them is eating apples."

I took the apple core from him. "They took the Ancients' apples."

"S'pose it's too much to ask that the Ancients get to 'em first."

We heard a growl and then a huff come out of the canyon. Ike pulled out his pistol. Like a dang fool, I left my Pa's army issue hanging from my saddle horn. Whatever made the sound was headed our way. The huffing got louder. Ike raised his gun and then settled down a bit when we heard another growl.

"Hold on," he said. "I think that's…"

Bob come running out of the shade of the canyon. He looked as happy as a pup running to its owner.

"Good God, Bob!" Ike said. "Look here, Henry, it's Bob!"

"I hope he ain't hungry," I said moving behind Ike.

"If he is," Ike said with a smile, "what say we feed him a couple of fucking marauders?"

"Fine by me," I said returning the smile.

***

Ike tossed the last of his cigarette to the ground as we approached Two Notch from the East. I couldn't see him, but Ike assured me that Bob was following us. Just as Abel had predicted, there were two fellas guarding the road into town. They were young, seventeen, maybe eighteen years old. Both of them small and boney.

"You remember Abel's instructions?" I asked.

Ike nodded, and I could tell he was scared out of his mind.

"Shoot the first one that speaks."

"Yeah, I know." He hiccupped. "Shit."

"Whatcha doing?"

"I get the hiccups when I'm really nervous."

"But you smoked one of your cigarettes. Ain't that supposed to calm you?"

"Sometimes. Sometimes it makes me a bit paranoid about the world. Right now, I think paranoid is winning the day. Oh shit."

"Work on letting it calm you," I said.

"I can't do that. It don't work that way. Oh Lord… I think I'm peeing myself."

I looked over at his crotch. "It don't appear like you are."

"Good, okay. It does that sometimes too, makes you think you're peeing yourself when you ain't." He breathed in through his nose and then jerked his head to his left. "What was that? Did you hear that? I heard something."

"I didn't hear nothing. These cigarettes make you hear things too?"

"Yeah, yeah. It's part of the paranoid thing. For instance, I'm pretty sure there's a hundred or so men out in the dark just waiting for us. Oh my God, this is so stupid."

"Ike," I said. "There ain't a hundred men out there. There ain't nobody out there."

"Really?"

"Really, I wouldn't lie to you."

"Oh shit. Oh shit. Oh shit."

"What?"

"Well, now I've got this voice in my head that's saying only a person who would lie to me would say 'I wouldn't lie to you.'"

I shook my head. "Take a deep breath. Remember shoot the first one that talks."

He took a breath and held it.

The two fellas got off their bony asses and walked to the middle of the road. One hugged a scatter gun and the other was belted up with two side arms. They stood their ground and stared at us.

We stopped ten feet from them. Ike was still holding his breath.

The fellas stared.

Ike held his breath.

The fellas stared.

Ike blew out the breath. "Ain't one of you going to say nothing."

The two fellas looked at each other and then the one with the scatter gun said, "What do you want us to say?"

Ike's eyes got big. His nostrils flared. He did a half turn my way and then busted out laughing. I ain't never heard somebody laugh so hard. "Oh my God," he said with a screech. "Oh my God! Did you hear the sound of his voice? Oh my God!"

Confused, I said, "No."

"No?" He was leaning over, red faced, laughing his heart out. "How could you not think that's funny?"

"What's wrong with my voice?" The fella with the scatter gun asked.

"There it is again!" He fell off his saddle and landed with a thud on the dirt, laughing even harder when he hit the ground.

"Look, here, fat-ass, I don't take to you making fun of me."

"Stop it!" Ike said. "You're killing me!"

Abel's plan was done in by one of Ike's cigarettes. It was pretty clear Ike wasn't going to shoot the fella. I tried to ready my Pa's army issue without getting noticed.

I seen a flash of brown to my left and then heard a horrible scream, followed by a roar and the sounds of bones crunching. By the time I got my wits about me to figure out what was going on, Bob had near tore the leg off the fella with the scatter gun. The fella with the side arms was backing away fumbling to unholster his guns.

"Bob's here," Ike said still laughing.

The fella with the side arms freed one of his guns and fired on Bob, but missed him by a mile.

"Hey," Ike said pulling his pistol out. In one smooth motion, he aimed and pulled the trigger. The bullet struck the fella with the side arms in the forehead, and he dropped like a sack of rocks.

I sat on my horse too shocked and confused to move.

"Damn," Ike said. "That wasn't the fella who talked first."

"We've made a mess of this, that's for sure," I said.

Bob was still going at the fella with the scatter gun. He'd stopped screaming, but I couldn't tell if he was dead or not. If he wasn't, he soon would be.

"What do we do?" I asked.

"I ain't wrestling that one away from Bob, that's for sure. Help me with the other one."

I jumped off my horse and helped him lift the man with the head wound and drape him over Ike's horse. Climbing into his saddle, he said, "They're ain't one to run back and tell him what I done, but it'll have to do."

I sat in my saddle. "What do we say happened to the other fella?

"He run off like a coward." As we rode by the giant bear tearing the man apart, Ike said, "Stay here, Bob."

The bear looked up at us and stuck out his blood soaked muzzle.

"Guess he was hungry," Ike said.

***

The noise of Two Notch crept out at us as we got closer to the center of town. There was laughing and screaming and just general mayhem somewheres in town. We steered the horses through the cracked streets and around garbage and the rusted out metal hulls my Pa called cars. I could see a rich amber glow through the spaces between the tumbledown houses. Something was burning.

When we hit Main Street, I got my first eyeful of the commotion. There was a raging party gathered around a bonfire. The townspeople were standing around stiff as sticks, but a group of drunk men was hopping around, drinking from whiskey bottles and firing their guns in the air. And, there in the middle of them, smiling bigger than shit was Old Kelly.

"You on your game?" I asked Ike.

He nodded. "Yeah, yeah. I think the foolishness has left me. I'm straight. I can do this."

"You sure?"

"No, but we can't turn back now."

I looked at him and realized he still had on the stupid ten gallon hat. "Get rid of your hat," I said.

"What?"

"The hat. Abel Decker wouldn't wear nothing like that."

"Oh, right." He ripped if off his head and tossed it behind a pile of trash.

Our horses ambled up just outside the circle of town folks. A few people noticed me and a chain of whispers started spreading the word we was there. The noise started to die down as each head turned our way.

One of the marauders spotted us and ran to a man standing next to Old Kelly.

The man stepped out from the others and everything went dead silent 'cept for the crackling of the bonfire. He was a broad man. His face was scarred up and down. His salt and pepper hair was slicked back drawing a good bit of the attention to his square chin.

We rode up.

"Well thank the heavens above," Old Kelly said. "Young Henry Arnaught. You ain't dead."

"No, ma'am, I'm not. Where's my Pa?"

"He's around."

"You him?" the man with the chin asked Ike.

"I am," he said sounding downright confident. "And you are?"

"Theodore Harding. That name mean anything to you?"

"Nope." Ike lifted the dead man up and pitched him off his horse. The body smacked the ground. "But I believe this is yours, Theodore."

Harding looked at the body. "I see the things they say about you are true."

"That depends what they say."

"They say you're a heartless demon that lives to kill."

"Then they say the truth," Ike said. He was sitting tall in his saddle, and I could tell he was crazy proud of himself.

"I've been waiting a long time for this, Abel Decker."

"You have?" Ike asked almost breaking character.

"You have no idea."

"I ain't got no interest either. I'm feeling generous tonight, so I'm willing to not spill anymore blood. Round up your men and leave."

Harding furrowed his brow and then laughed. "What are you talking about?"

Ike looked at me sideways and cleared his throat. "I was hired by the town to deal with you and your men. Like I said, I'm feeling generous…"

Harding slapped his leg and busted out laughing even louder. "Abel Decker, you are as dumb as you are mean."

"Wha… what is that supposed to mean?" Ike asked.

"You weren't hired by the town to deal with us. We hired the town to lure you here so we could deal with you."

"What… no… wait… Really?" Ike was flustered. His face had turned beet red. He looked at me. "Is that true?"

"No, sir," I said. "It ain't. Old Kelly had the vision…"

"About that," Old Kelly said. "This wasn't a religious vision as much as it was a business agreement I made with Mr. Harding here."

"You lied?" I asked.

"I don't lie," Old Kelly said. "I make necessary adjustments to the truth in order to bring hope and happiness to the good people of Two Notch. Mr. Harding made a sizeable donation to our town's kitty in exchange for our assistance in getting Abel Decker here."

Ike gritted his teeth. "I don't understand."

"Welcome to your ambush," Harding said with this arms spread wide. "You see, I felt it would be just a tad foolish to face you on your home turf, so I wanted to find a neutral out-of-the-way spot to face you."

"Face me for what?"

"My name, Mr. Decker. Harding. That doesn't mean anything to you?"

"I told you before it don't."

"Where's my Pa?" I asked again.

"Shut up, boy," Harding said. "The grownups are talking."

"Why should your name mean anything to me?"

"My brother's name was Wilson Harding. He served with you in the 183rd."

"I served with a lot of people."

"I imagine you did. The great Abel Decker. The war hero. The finest example of this country's idea of a soldier. You fought for us. You killed for us. You, sir, are the patron saint of holy terror."

"What does this have to do with your brother?"

"I'm getting to that. Your myth has its dark side, Mr. Decker. What people won't say about you is that you didn't fight for this country. You fought for Abel Decker. You killed for Abel Decker."

"Oh my God," Ike said. "Does this story have an end?"

"You killed my brother in the war, you son-of-a-bitch!" His voice echoed through the streets of Two Notch.

Ike stammered and worked to collect himself. "Things like that happen in war. It's called friendly fire…"

"I'm not an idiot, Mr. Decker. I know what friendly fire is, and this was no case of friendly fire. You and one other man were the only ones to survive in a twenty man patrol of a hostile town on the Southeast perimeter of the front line. Just two of you. The official report was so fucking sanitized I knew it was bullshit. So I spent eighteen years tracking down the other man who survived, and he told me what really happened that day. Now, I want you to tell me."

"I served sixteen years of combat duty, Mr. Harding. Details elude me."

Harding pulled a gun and fired, hitting Ike in the arm.

Ike barked out in pain and twisted in his saddle.

"Stop!" I said. "He ain't Abel Decker!"

"Shut up!" Ike said clutching his arm.

"What the hell you mean, boy?"

"Leave it, Henry," Ike said. "I can handle this."

"What does the boy mean?" Harding asked.

"He's just trying to protect me. Don't pay him any mind. I'm Abel Decker."

Harding aimed his gun at Ike's head. "Then tell me what happened to my brother."

Ike groaned. "It's like you said. I killed your brother."

"How?"

"I can't remember."

Harding moved the gun down and shot Ike in the other arm. Ike dropped off his horse.

"He ain't Abel!" I said placing my hand on my Pa's army issue.

Harding turned his gun on me. "Don't be stupid, boy."

I quickly removed my hand. "You gotta listen to me."

Ike was flat on his back, rocking from side to side. Spit and curse words was flying from his mouth.

"Talk," Harding said to me.

"He ain't Abel Decker. He's his brother Ike. I swear it's the truth."

Harding looked disappointed as hell and madder than shit at the news. "Where's Abel?"

"Dead. Left for anyway. He got gut shot in Cannibal Orchard. When we left him, he was on his last."

"Gut shot by who?"

"A boy cannibal. Abel killed the boy's daddy, so the boy gunned him down for it."

Harding smiled and then broke out in a steady creepy laugh. "The great Abel Decker gunned down by a boy. If that ain't something to scratch your head about. Where is this boy? I'd like to shake his hand."

"Can't," I said. "I killed him."

His laugh picked up. "That's a damn shame." He turned to his men. "Drag the fat imposter to town hall."

"There ain't no call to hurt Ike," I said. "Abel's gone."

"I've got call," Harding said. "In fact, this is more poetic. A brother for a brother. I tell you what. The report said my brother died from a bullet wound in the back of the head at 3:36 in the afternoon. I say we perfect this poetry and kill the fat man tomorrow at 3:36 on the dot."

Two of Harding's dirt-covered scoundrels yanked Ike up by his arms to torture him. They jerked him around while they dragged him off.

"I'm warning you," I said without an ounce of authority, "if you kill Ike, I'll make you pay."

Harding sneered. "That's big talk for a pint-sized killer. Well, if you're threatening to make me pay for killing the worthless likes of Abel Decker's brother, I can't imagine what you're going to say when you find out I killed your daddy."

A mad humming filled my ears. Every bit of sound on the planet seemed to come at me at once. I felt my heart slow and thump against my chest. I wanted to go back in time to right before Harding said what he said. I was sure I didn't hear him right. He didn't just say he killed my Pa.

"Fucker got wind of our arrangement with Old Kelly. Set off on foot to find you. Caught up to him just outside of Besser Pass. Brought him back. Consulted with your rector on how to handle him. She convinced us that he wouldn't give up on the idea of trying to reach you, and I got too much on my mind to babysit a determined father, so we had a proper hanging two streets over."

"You killed my Pa?" My eyelids got heavy, and I was struggling to keep them up.

"It's a shame, too. From what I hear, he was an honest to goodness war hero, unlike Abel Decker."

"You're lying. You're just trying to get me to lift up on you."

"See for yourself. We left him strung up to serve as a reminder to the rest of the folks that I didn't have the time to babysit none of them either."

My throat started to burn.

"I'll give you an escort and everything." He turned and yelled, "Willie!"

A boy just a few years older than me run forward, "Yeah, Pa."

"Take this young man to his daddy so he can pay his respects."

Willie looked up at me. "Can I have his gun?"

"Don't see why not." Harding held his hand up to me and motioned with his fingers for me to hand it over.

I thought about shooting him, but he'd get off a shot before I even got my finger on the trigger.

***

My Pa swung in the breeze and one hand grasped the rope around his neck. His feet pointed up, which I took to mean he fought to the very end. His skin was blue.

I sat on my horse while Willie held the reins. My Pa's army issue was hung around his shoulder. We were alone at the end of Wayne Archer Lane. The noise of the celebration carried on behind us.

"When did you hang him?" I asked.

"Two days ago." He reached in his pocket and pulled out an apple. "Cried like a baby. Begged us not to do it."

"Be careful, Willie," I said.

He laughed like his father. "Shut up, you little puke. What are you going to do about it?"

"I won't have to do nothing."

"What's that supposed to mean?"

"It means I know where you got that apple."

He looked at the fruit. "What of it?"

"You shouldn't have took 'em."

"We take what we want." He bit into the apple again.

"And you'll be judged for it."

He giggled and chewed on his apple. "I hope my daddy lets me cut your throat."

I peered into the darkness beyond the tree my Pa hung from and saw the lantern eyes staring back.

"You're not going to get the chance."

He shook his head. "You're touched, boy. Got bats in your brain."

"I want you to know something," I said seeing three more sets of eyes shine through the darkness.

"What?"

"I'm going to kill your Pa."

He almost choked on his apple. "You're good at making jokes..."

"It ain't a joke."

"What makes you think I ain't going to just point this gun of yours and pull the trigger. That'll be the end of that."

"You won't have the chance."

"Lord, stop with your tough guy bullshit, kid. It's tiring."

"I ain't going to do nothing to you, Willie. They will." I pointed to the growing number of eyes in the darkness.

He stumbled back and raised the gun. I slapped my horse on the behind, and he kicked up, knocking Willie to the ground. In a flash, I was off the horse and holding the gun.

"Get up," I said.

He stood with a huff. "You ain't gonna shoot."

"No, I ain't. Not unless you run."

"What is it then? I'm your hostage?"

"Nope." I stepped toward him and he stepped back.

"What are you going to do?"

"Nothing. Just turn around and walk."

The lantern eyes were growing bigger as they moved in closer.

"They your gang?"

"Nope. Walk." I pushed the barrel of the gun into his back and shoved him.

He slowly moved toward the eyes.

"Who are they?"

"They're your ghosts, Willie. Go and face 'em."

"I can talk to my Pa," he said. "Maybe save the fat fella."

"Don't need you for that. I'll save him."

"You don't know my Pa. He ain't reasonable. Got a mean streak in him a mile wide. He won't listen to nobody but me." He was standing in the grass just past my Pa when he turned to me. "I was lying about your daddy. He fought like hell to get loose and look for you. He didn't beg a bit."

"I know. You ain't gotta tell me that."

The Ancients got close enough so I could hear their whispering.

"C'mon, boy! Please..."

"I ain't a boy."

Three Ancients sprang out of the dark and leapt on Willie. He screamed bloody murder as they carried him into the night. I seen a couple of the Ancients' dogs bounding through the dead grass.

"Hey!" I heard a voice call out.

Three of Harding's men approached from the other end of the street on horseback.

I fired a shot their way to disburse them and then climbed on the back of my horse. Before I rode out I vowed to my Pa that I would be back to cut him down.

***

I rode through the darkness as fast as my horse could go. The three men were in pursuit, but my size gave my horse less weight to carry, so I was able to increase my distance. Even still, I kicked and screamed at my horse to go faster.

I'd lost my way in the dark. My plan was to head for Besser Pass and hope that they wouldn't be fool enough to follow me. I wasn't sure if the Ancients would allow me in the canyon at night, but I had nothing to lose by taking my chances.

I spotted the rise of the cliffs ahead and asked my horse for even more speed. And he give it to me. So fast that the world turned to a blur. Rocks, brush, tumbleweed, they all blended in with the brown and red dirt that surrounded me.

I seen a flash of blue at one point and didn't give it much thought. Then a small flash of pink. I turned to see what I had just passed. A pop sounded off, and one of the three horsemen fell from his horse. Another pop and another horseman down. A third pop and the last horseman still rode. The forth pop saw the man go down.

I pulled my horse to a stop and wheeled him around. A woman was hooting and hollering.

Miss Connie.

I jumped from my horse. "Miss Connie?"

"I got 'em!" There was nothing but pure joy in her voice.

I found my way to her. "What are you doing here?"

"Did you see?" She asked. "Shot three of 'em with four shots. That's not bad."

"No, ma'am, it ain't bad at all. But what are you doing here? Did Abel pass?"

"Not yet."

I looked to my left and there stood Abel Decker with Doreen's help. The pink I thought I saw was his blood-soaked shirt.

"What in the world…"

"Couldn't talk him out of it," Miss Connie said. "He bugged the living shit out of us until we propped him on his horse and come this way. Left about two hours after you and... Where's Ike?"

I couldn't answer.

"Where is he, Henry?" Abel asked.

"It was a set up. The whole thing. Old Kelly didn't have no vision. She got paid off by Harding to trick you into coming to Two Notch where he could get his revenge on you for killing his brother in the war."

"Killing his brother?" Abel said. "Harding?" He mulled the name over. "His brother Wilson Harding?"

"You remember him?"

"I do," Abel said hobbling towards me using Doreen as a support system. "I killed him all right. Shot him in the back of the head like the coward he was. Sonny-bitch led us into an ambush. Took us right into the teeth of the enemy in exchange for money and whores. No offense, Miss Connie."

"None taken."

"They shot up Ike," I said. "I told'em you were dead. I wasn't lying to 'em. I thought you was dead the way we left ya'."

"I will be soon enough. Turns out them cannibals had some effective pain stoppers Miss Connie found. My guts are leaking blood inside, but it don't hurt a bit."

"Is Ike dead?" Miss Connie asked.

"No, ma'am. Not yet. They're planning on shooting him in the back of the head at 3:36 tomorrow. Same way and same time Abel done in Harding's brother."

"That's a hell of thing," Abel said.

"What should we do?" I asked.

"Got enough of them drugs to last until morning?" Abel asked Miss Connie.

She dug through her pocket and pulled out two yellow pills. "Just enough."

"Then provided I don't bleed to death by then, we'll wait 'til morning and spring Ike then."

"Why morning? Why not now?"

"Cause I ain't going to be at my best in this fight. I need them liquored up and sloppy. We'll let them have the night. We'll take the morning. You and your Pa will have your town back by noon."

"My Pa's…" a lump caught the words in my throat. I cleared them through and spit it out. "My Pa's dead. Hung him in the streets for everyone to see."

"Oh, honey," Miss Connie said reaching out for me, but I pulled away before she could hug me.

"All respect, Miss Connie, but it ain't time for that. I'd like to keep hold of this mad 'til our work's done."

She nodded.

"Why don't you gals retrieve them fella's guns and ammo. I want to talk to Henry."

Doreen and Connie hurried towards the fallen horsemen.

"Sit," Abel said as he eased himself down on the ground.

I sat across from him.

"Your Pa wouldn't want you having no part of what's gotta be done tomorrow."

"My Pa's dead."

"Don't make him any less your Pa."

"I'm gonna kill Theodore Harding, Abel."

"You need to let me do that, son."

"Why? It was my Pa that he killed."

"'Cause if you do happen to find a way to kill the man it's gonna change you. You won't never be the same."

"I already killed that boy."

"That was different. That was out of anger. You lost yourself for a minute."

"I'm angry now. More."

"I know, but still you wouldn't be killing Harding for the same reason."

"I don't see no difference."

"The difference is you think that killing Harding will give you some kind of peace, and it won't. Not even close. Once you see that, you ain't gonna ever find peace again. You'll be as dead inside as I've been for most of my life."

"I thought you said I needed to be a killer."

"I was wrong about that. Took a bullet in the belly for me to find my permanent high tide, son. You don't need to be nothing like me."

A growl drew our attention away from the conversation. Bob lumbered toward us. His mouth was still covered in blood. He stopped and stretched out on the dirt ten feet from us.

"Goddamn bear," Abel said. "Promise me one thing, Henry."

"Yes, sir."

"Don't let that fucker eat me when I die."

***

I woke up to Abel staring down at me from his horse. His face was pale 'cept for black circles under his eyes. He coughed until I thought he'd hack up his innards. "I've decided that today ain't about killing."

"Sir?"

"It's about getting Ike out of that town of yours."

"Yes, sir."

"I'll change out with Ike. They'll take me for him."

"Ain't gonna be that simple."

"Why not?"

"Harding's boy got took by the Ancients last night. Weren't nobody around, but me. He's liable to put the blame on me."

Abel flinched and grabbed at his belly.

"You alright?"

"I seen better days. The pills are wearing off." He forced himself to sit tall in his saddle. "Ancients? The boy take the apples from the pass?"

"Not sure if it was him, but someone in Harding's gang did."

"That works in our favor then. We ain't the only ones going up against Harding."

"But they won't show 'til dark. They're set to kill Ike at 3:36."

He bent over and held his breath.

"Anything I can do?"

"Yeah, get on your horse and switch out firearms with me."

"What for?"

"Gun's too damn big for you, and I've had plenty of practice using it."

I retrieved the gun and handed it up to him. He pulled his pistol from his jacket and gave it to me.

"Never thought I'd use one of these again," Abel said.

I climbed on my horse and was about to coax him forward when it hit me that something was missing. "Where's Miss Connie and Doreen?

"They rode ahead. Harding's likely relaxed since he thinks I'm dead. Sentries won't be posted. Your town's folks will be too frazzled and scared to pay any mind to two female strangers. The gals got a better chance of riding into town without notice than us. They can get inside and scope things out. We're set to meet up with them at noon at the West entrance into town."

"That's smart."

"Not my first time doing this sort of thing."

We rode towards Two Notch at a slow pace so as not to jostle Abel around too much.

"Okay," he said, "here's what we'll do. I took Harding's boy, understand?"

"Yes, sir."

"We'll use him as a bargaining chip."

"But you didn't really take him."

"Harding don't know that. If he thinks I got him, I can stall him on killing Ike until dark. Give our green-eyed friends a chance to get in on the action."

"But…" I stopped myself. I had reservations about his plan, but he was Abel Decker. I didn't feel it was my place to question his wisdom.

"What?"

"Nothing."

"Go on, Henry. You got something to say, say it."

I hesitated and then said, "Well, sir. There's a couple things I ain't too sure about. The Ancients, they seem to come when they come. They ain't on a regular hunting schedule. They could have had me and Doreen that first night we took the apples, but they never even tried."

"Probably because they were feasting on that horse of yours. Meals like that are a rarity to them."

"Maybe, but seems like a big gamble. You're going to make Harding even madder by claiming to have his boy. Liable to put him in a fit of desperation. Shoot you on the spot."

"Nah, he'll want the boy. He ain't getting him if I'm dead."

"Well, sir, if you'll excuse me for saying so, that's my other concern. I got my doubts you're going to survive the ride into Two Notch much less hold out 'til dark."

He wheezed out a chuckle. "That's a sensible concern." He winked and said, "The plan's the plan, young Henry. Nothing left to discuss."

We rode in silence until we reached the outskirts of Two Notch. Smoke choked the little town. Abel was hunched over and it was hard to tell if his eyes were closed. I reached out to touch him, half expecting to find out he was dead, but he spoke instead.

"I'm alive." He stretched his neck and surveyed Two Notch. "Forgot what a shithole it is."

Two riders approached. One was slight and tall. The other was a little girl. Miss Connie and Doreen. Only Miss Connie was dressed in the clothes of one of the men she shot the night before, and Doreen was riding one or their horses.

"Good, you're here," Miss Connie said.

"Is it noon?" Abel asked.

"Not even close," she said.

"What the hell you doing here then? You're supposed to be scouting out the situation."

"We did and it isn't good."

"What's wrong?" I asked.

"Harding's gone crazy. His boy's missing, and he's doing a house-to-house search for him right now. I saw him shoot a woman. His men are burning everything in their wake. It's bad."

"How many men?"

"Seven on the streets including Harding. One watching over Ike in the town hall."

"Anything I need to know about your rector?" he asked me.

"She's got men, too. Half dozen. They're piss-shit stupid, though, and they ain't well-armed."

"What do we do?" Miss Connie asked.

"Henry and I will ride into town and make a proposal. You and the girl stay here."

"What? No. You need more guns." She and Doreen both pulled out the pistols they took from the dead horsemen.

"I need them tonight. Don't want to show my hand right now."

"Then I should go with you and Henry will stay with Doreen."

"Nope."

"Why?"

"Cause I said so, damn it. You forget who's in command," he said with a grin. He propped the butt of my Pa's army issue against his thigh, and we headed for Two Notch.

***

It wasn't hard to find Harding. He was yelling up a storm beating the hell out of Tate Crawford. I didn't care for Tate, but I couldn't help but feel bad for him for taking the beating Harding was throwing down on him.

Harding threw a punch into poor Tate's ribs and stepped back, catching sight of us as he did. "Boy?"

The muscles in Abel's jaw drew tight and his knuckles turned white as he gripped his saddle horn. "His name's Henry."

"And you are?" Harding asked.

"Abel Decker."

Harding's face turned hot red. His mouth dropped open and a vein popped out on his forehead. "Abel Decker." He smiled. "Abel fucking Decker! I heard you were dead."

"I was, but I come back to deal with the brother of that shit-box traitor Wilson Harding. Would that be you?"

His smile disappeared. "Watch what you say? Wilson was a goddamn patriot and hero."

"Wilson was a turncoat, and best thing I ever done for my country was put a bullet in the back of his head."

He turned to one of his men. "Give me your gun!"

Abel pointed Pa's gun at Harding. "Let's not get into that just yet."

"I ain't about to listen to your foul bullshit. I'm going to shoot you down, Abel Decker. Right here and right now. Then I'm going to kill your brother. Just like you killed mine."

"You do that, and you ain't never going to see your boy."

Harding cocked his head. "What?"

"You heard me. I got your boy."

"You son-of-a-bitch…"

"Save it. Here's how it's going to work. Your boy for my brother."

Harding stood silent for a while and then stomped the ground. "You ain't gonna ruin this for me. I aim to kill you for what you done to my brother…"

"You'll get your chance, but not until your boy and my brother are out of the picture."

"You'll give yourself over?"

"I will."

He huffed and grunted. "Goddamn it! I don't like this. I can't trust you."

"Then we ain't got nothing left to discuss." He urged his horse back.

"Where you going?"

"To kill your boy," Abel said as matter of fact as someone announcing he was tired.

"Wait," Harding said. "I get my boy and you for your brother?"

"Those are the terms."

"Agreed."

"Fine. We'll make the exchange just after dark at the head of Besser Pass."

"Besser Pass?"

"That's what I said."

"No, we'll do it here in front of town hall."

"We won't. We'll do it at Besser Pass." Abel scanned the crowd of people that had gathered. "Now if you'd point out Old Kelly to me, I'd be obliged."

"What do you want with Old Kelly?" Harding asked.

"We've got business," Abel said.

I pointed to Old Kelly who was standing between Buster and another one of her goons in front of the crowd. "That's her."

She stepped forward and smiled nervously. "God be with you Abel Decker…"

A loud bang cut her off. I seen a streak of smoke come out of the muzzle of my Pa's army issue. I watched as if time was stuck in honey as a bullet went through Old Kelly's eye and blew out the back her head.

Buster stumbled back covered in Old Kelly's brains and blood. A girlish whimpering come out of his mouth before he passed clean out. As gruesome as the sight of it was, I smiled at the sight of Buster losing his knees.

Abel rested the butt of the gun back on his thigh. "That going to be a problem?" he asked Harding.

Harding was the only one who hadn't ducked at the sound of the shot. He shrugged and said, "Nope. Seems fair."

***

Abel leaned up against a rock at the foot of Besser Mountain and fought for a good clean breath. If I'd just come up on him without knowing his circumstances, I would have guessed he was covered in white paint. I didn't see no part of his skin that looked natural. I couldn't figure how in the hell he was keeping himself alive.

The sun was dipping and night would be on us soon enough. I asked Abel a few hours before what the plan was and all he said was to let him think on it. I'd given up hope he had formulated one until he groaned out, "How big was this boy?"

"Bigger than me," I said. "I reckon he was about fifteen or sixteen."

"How'd he compare to Miss Connie?"

I looked Miss Connie over and she stood up straight to give me a good representation of her build. "Well, Willie didn't have none of her bumps or curves, but they're about the same height and weight I guess."

"Miss Connie," Abel said, "you're gonna get your chance at killing some dick slingers after all."

She smiled.

I shook my head. "You figure on passing off Miss Connie as Willie?"

"It'll be darker tonight. The moon's been shrinking the last few nights. Hat'll cover her face. Coat'll cover the bumps and curves."

"It ain't gonna work," I said.

"It'll buy us enough time."

"There's gotta be something else we can do…"

"Henry," Miss Connie said, "Leave it. It's the best plan we've got."

"You and the girl will wait on the pass."

"The pass? But we can't get off good shots from there."

"This thing goes sour your best bet is to hightail it into the canyon."

"But we can shoot!" I said not knowing if Doreen had the first idea on how to shoot, but I wasn't going to be left out of the fight.

"Son!" Abel yelled. The power of his voice surprised me. I didn't think he had that much strength left in him. "This is how it's gonna be!" His eyes rolled back in his head for a split second, but he willed them back down. "Understood?"

I could have argued with him, but I was afraid the argument would kill him, so I just nodded and waited for the sun to fall.

***

They come riding all in a row, nine men on horses. It was so dark I couldn't make out none of their faces. That was good because that meant they were met with the same issue when it come to Abel and Miss Connie.

The two of them stood with the pass to their backs. Miss Connie laced her fingers together in front of her. Her head was hung low. She wore one of the dead horsemen's coat and hat. I hoped I was right about her size being close to Willie's.

The horses stopped and eight of the men dismounted. The husky fella in the middle sat on his mount slumped over. I figured right away it was Ike. The two men closest to him yanked him off his perch.

Harding yelled across the blackness, "Willie?"

Miss Connie dropped her head lower.

"The boy can't talk," Abel said.

"Why not?

"I broke his jaw for being a Harding, you gutless bastard!"

"Look here! You didn't have no cause to do him like that!"

"The hell I didn't! You shot my brother up!"

There was a pause. "Still, he's just a boy!"

"Are we gonna spend all night yapping or are we gonna get to this thing?"

"Bring the boy over if you're in such a God awful hurry!"

"Send my brother over first," Abel said.

"You think I trust you…"

"Fine, will meet in the middle."

Harding walked over to Ike and said something to the men next to him. "I'm sending two of my men out with your brother."

"Fine." Abel attempted to take a step but stumbled and fell to a knee. Miss Connie reached out to help him stand, but he slapped her hand away. "They see you help me they'll know something's up." He stood back up.

"You drunk, Abel Decker?" Harding asked.

Abel stood. "There a law against it?" He grabbed Miss Connie's arm and they started walking toward the line of gunmen.

The two men standing next to Ike grabbed him without an ounce of concern for his wounds and manhandled him forward. He barked in pain.

The distance between both sides shrank painfully slow. I found myself lurching forward trying to get a better view through the darkness. Doreen was doing the same.

Finally, they reached each other. Miss Connie still had her head down. I could hear Ike whimpering.

"Leave go of my brother," Abel said.

Miss Connie lifted her head.

"Hey," the man on Ike's left said. "This ain't…"

Miss Connie pulled a hunting knife from her coat sleeve and jammed it into the man's throat.

The man on Ike's right stepped back pointing his gun at Miss Connie.

Abel shot him before he took his second step.

All hell broke loose after that. Ike dropped to the ground while Miss Connie and Abel got off as many shots as they could. Harding's men were slow to react. Two more went down before they started returning fire. The darkness gave Miss Connie and Abel enough cover that the returning fire missed wildly at first. But before long, I heard a whack. Miss Connie cried out and fell back on her ass. Her hat flew off.

Doreen took off running toward her.

"Doreen, get back here!" I said.

She paid me no mind and zipped through the darkness right into the middle of it all.

I felt a second of relief when I seen another one of Harding's men drop. It was just three of them left now, and I let myself believe that Abel Decker was actually going to win the day on this one. His legend was going to be even bigger.

Another whack!

Abel stood up straight, clutched his chest and then fell to his knees. A beat later, he hit the dirt face first.

The shooting stopped.

Doreen screamed when she reached Miss Connie. She dropped to the ground next to her and tugged on her coat.

Ike wasn't moving. I couldn't' tell if he'd been shot again, but it was clear that he wasn't getting up anytime soon.

Harding and his men walked up on Abel with their guns drawn.

"He ain't moving," one man said.

"Don't mean he's dead," Harding said. "Roll him over."

His men holstered their guns and used all their strength to roll Abel over on his back.

"He's dead," the one closest to Abel said.

As soon as the word 'dead' left his mouth, Abel sat up and shoved a knife in the man's ear and then fired a bullet right in the middle of the other man's chest.

Harding fired six shots, hitting Abel with every one.

I looked down at my Pa's army issue and said to myself, "Red is for ammo. Blue is for pulse." With that, I pulled one of the batteries from my pocket and loaded it into the gun.

Harding roared like a madman. "Where is my boy?"

A rock struck him on the chin and he howled in pain.

Doreen had her arm cocked back ready to throw another one, but Harding regained his senses and turned his gun on her.

I stood and said, "No!"

Harding and Doreen both looked at me.

"I'll take you to your boy!"

"Who's that?" Harding said trying to get his eyes on me through the dark.

"Henry Arnaught!"

Harding started walking towards me.

I slipped back deeper into the canyon.

"Don't play games with me, boy."

"You want your son back?"

He came closer and I sank back into the mouth of the canyon.

"Goddamn it! Stop!"

"It's this way," I said.

He reached the edge of the pass and stopped.

"Bring him here."

"Can't."

"Why not?"

I thought for minute. "'Cause he can't walk, and I ain't big enough to carry him."

"Where is he?"

I pointed to a pile of rocks on the left side of the canyon. "Over there."

He narrowed his eyes. "Where?"

"Behind those rocks."

"If you're lying to me, boy, I'll hang you by your toes and bleed you like a pig."

He headed for the pile of rocks.

I moved to the other side of the canyon. When his back was turned, I raised my gun and pointed it at him.

He reached the rocks and turned in a fit of anger when he didn't find Willie. "Boy!"

"Henry," I said.

He saw the gun and he held up his arms. "You ain't gonna shoot me, are you?"

I shook my head. "No, sir. Not the way you think anyway."

He chuckled. "What other way is there?"

"Well, this here's an AR-15 Pulse-3 rifle. Army issue. Belonged to my Pa. The fella you strung up in the street."

"I was just doing what was necessary."

"And this here's necessary. You see, red is for ammo and blue is for pulse."

"I am familiar with the gun."

"Good. Saves me anymore explaining."

We stood for a few moments in silence.

"Well, are you going to shoot me or not?"

"I'm waiting."

"For what?"

A set of green eyes appeared on the canyon wall just above Harding.

"Them," I said looking up.

Harding followed my line of sight and was startled to see the lantern eyes looking down at him. "What is that?"

"I ain't gonna kill ya' because like Abel said, it won't bring me peace. But the way I figure, there ain't nothing wrong with me making sure you answer for what you took from the Ancients."

"What did I take?"

I pulled the blue trigger and a bright flash of light shot out of the muzzle. It traveled like a wave and struck down Harding. He wasn't dead, but it cold cocked the hell out of him. "You took their apples," I said walking away.

By the time I walked out of the canyon I got great satisfaction out of hearing Theodore Harding screaming for his life.

16

We buried Abel on his property near where the horses grazed. It was a breezy day with just a hint of a mist in the air. We didn't say a prayer over him because Abel wouldn't have looked too kindly on that. We just stood without uttering a word for the longest time.

Ike eventually broke the silence and bent down towards me. Abel's dog tags dangled from his neck. Both his arms were wrapped to his chest. "Do me a favor and set these dog tags on the grave for me."

I did as he asked.

"Doesn't anyone want to say anything?" Miss Connie asked. Her long red coat covered up her bandaged midsection. She took a bullet in the side that missed all her insides and exited her back.

Doreen stood beside her dressed in the same coat. They made a fine looking pair, a mother with her new daughter.

In fact, they looked like a picture perfect family. Ike finally got the female companionship he was looking for. Miss Connie didn't have much interest in whoring no more, and Ike needed looking after until he mended. She agreed to stick around long as he kept his advances down to a minimum.

Doreen didn't have no reason to stay in Two Notch. Old Kelly's law wasn't in effect no more, but the sentiment about barren girls wasn't likely to change overnight. She was better off under Miss Connie's watch.

I didn't have no choice, but to stay in Two Notch. It really was a shithole, but it was my shithole. Besides, someone had to look for the yield in the dirt now that my Pa was dead.

"What do you say about a man that was a mean son-of-a-bitch most his life?" Ike said.

"Don't you have any good memories of your brother?" Connie said.

Ike gave it some thought and then shook his head. "Can't think of a single one. He was just mean. That's all he come to be anyway. He was good before the war, but I don't remember a thing about that Abel Decker."

"All I know is he took out those marauders," I said as I mounted my blonde horse with the black mane and tail.

"Fucking marauders," Ike said.

"Right," I said with a grin. "Fucking marauders. And more importantly he killed Old Kelly," I urged my horse along. "So, as far as I'm concerned, he's the man who saved Two Notch."

The End